W9-CHR-715

CHILDREN OF THE DAWN

Copyright © 1999 by Andrés Berger-Kiss

All rights reserved under International and Pan-American
Copyright Conventions.
Published in the United States by
Dancing Moon Press, Newport, Oregon
Distributed by Partners/West, Renton, Washington
Cover painting: Susan Adele Pasarow
"Fire Mountain"/AC 30"x22"
Cover design: Yalcin Erhan

Library of Congress Cataloging-in-Publication Data
98-74313
Berger-Kiss, Andrés
Children of the dawn / Andrés Berger-Kiss
ISBN 1-892076-06-3
I. Title.

Manufactured in the United States of America

FIRST EDITION

ANDRÉS BERGER–KISS

CHILDREN OF THE DAWN

DANCING MOON PRESS
NEWPORT, OREGON

ALSO BY ANDRÉS BERGER-KISS

Children of the Dawn (Novel)
Voices from the Earth = Voces de la Tierra
(Poetry)
Hijos de la Madrugada (Novel)
The Sharpener (Short Story)
Letters to My Lover (Short Story)
The Meeting (Short Story)
Don Alejandro y Sus 186 Hijos (Novel)
The Treasure Hunter (Short Story)
The Night I Met Lincoln (Short Story)

This work is dedicated to the native tribes
of the American continent
hoping the day is not far
when they will regain firm footing
on their trails.

Andrés Berger-Kiss, October 12, 1998

Contents

FIRST PART

I

THE BIRTH

SLOWLY, SHE BEGAN CLIMBING THE HILL. NO ONE noticed. Most of the women her age climbed the hill at least once a year and now it was her turn, her first time. She planned to climb it many times in her life.

If only she could have finished the work before the pains made it impossible to continue. But the pains had been great and had mounted in intensity as the day wore on. Now the sun was setting, shadows were lengthening and soon it would be dark. If she could not reach the lake in time, something bad could happen.

She did not want anything bad to happen. Not her first time.

Here was the path up the hill. If she followed it, the lake would be at the end, where one need not be afraid of evil because the moon was there, looking down. She would finish the work tomorrow.

Her feet dug into the dirt and she stopped a moment. Bending down, she picked up the dirt in her toes and rubbed it on her abdomen with her hand, under her skirt. This was good dirt. Dirt that made things grow.

Yes, tomorrow she would finish the roof. She had threaded it already with corn silk, made it thick with banana leaves and palms, made it strong by soaking all of it in the river and letting it dry under the sun, made it slick by pouring grease over it so the rain would not drip into the hut. All she had to do was tie it firmly to the ditch reed so the wind would not blow it down. She felt strong and free when thinking about the wind.

She looked back and saw the shadows closing in on her. She continued walking and after a while realized it was getting dark. She saw little spots of light as they touched the grass and the leaves in the trees.

Then she began to feel the pains again, even more intensely. But her face was still, and she did not complain. She lifted her skirt, rubbed more dirt on her abdomen and, looking down, said:

"Wait. Yet it is not the time."

And she thought she must hurry, for her load was impatient.

She began moving faster with her legs spread, holding her breath, sweating, tensing the muscles of her abdomen, biting into her lips until she felt blood run down her chin and something warmer run down the inside of her legs.

It was dark when she reached the top of the hill where she sat down beside the lake. It was light above, where the moon had come to meet her.

She rested a while, and when she could breathe more easily she reached for a few banana leaves and placed them on the humid ground, then found two large stones. Holding one stone in each hand she crouched on the banana leaves, facing the moon and spreading her legs. And looking into the face of the moon, thrusting her pelvis forward and squeezing the two stones into the earth, she cried in the night:

"Now is the time of the coming! Come! Come! Come!"

But the child would not come and she saw the moon looking down, eternal frozen wanderer of the purple space among the stars. She watched the moon until it was so pale she knew the dawn must arrive.

She saw the formless clouds were shaped by the winds, transformed into gigantic men that filled the whole sky, marching across the firmament, moving worlds, leaping over the flaming horizon.

Between the night and the dawn she heard her babe cry, and making a last effort, she pressed her hands against her abdomen where the good dirt lay so the blood there would flow freely into the new life. This was good blood, blood that made things grow. At last she gave birth. Then she rubbed the cord that held their lives together with the two stones. When the cord was broken and they were one no more, she felt relieved of her burden.

She examined the babe, touching it eagerly with her fingertips and felt the wild beating of her own heart, a beating that was now faster than ever before in her life. When she found that the child was a man, she smiled and looked up with tenderness at the pale moon.

She took the babe in her arms and walked into the waters of the lake, washing him well so the moon would admire him. She thought of the pride she would feel tying the roof onto the sticks of the hut with her babe on her back, with all the villagers gathered around, watching her, knowing that her first one was a man.

This was the beginning of a new day.

II
THE CONQUEST

MIST SLOWLY RISES WHEN THE EARLY SUN MOVES above the cordillera. Stand on one of the hills watching any of the rivers rush through the canyons until you lose sight of it in the immense jungles beyond, moving among the green vaults toward the sea, and if here is the place you were born, if on this part of earth you spent your youth, if your ancestors are buried by these hillsides, you will know with certainty that this land belongs to you.

You will see with the passage of time and the increasing warmth of the day how the mist vanishes and the vast fields clear, exhibiting their limitless beauty.

Toward the south, mountains leap out of the sea against the hostile Western winds. The mountains begin where the earth is cold, dark and deserted. At times, the hills surrender and fall against the sea forming cliffs and islands, but soon they rebel against the turbulent waters that do not let them surge, and moving into the arms of the continent they climb toward the sky, forming the most sovereign heights of the world. Should you go eastward, you will first see the savage pampas which extend into infinity.

If you walk toward the north, you will see impenetrable jungles, enmeshed with profound rivers. Later, much further North and West, by the warm oceans, by the beaches of soft sands where the horizons open, you will feel the sensuousness of the tropics in the fertile hillsides and in the valleys of incomparable beauty where you will be embraced by the mountains of your homeland with a touch no other place on earth can replicate.

Even as a stranger who has never seen this place, you will know with certainty that the road to a lovelier homeland does not exist; and if that earth were to sneak into your blood, you'd know you love her because the promise she makes is that of freedom.

But if you had lived here for a thousand years and could no longer tell your hand from the earth it clutches; if you had scraped the fertile ground with your daily sweat; if in your idolatry you had molded its clay to worship it; if your mother had rubbed it into your entrails even before your birth; and yet, neither your work, nor your love, nor your death could make the land yours, then not even sky, nor time, nor the gods, or the hundred loathsome plagues and wars whose torments and pestilence have been your daily companions, or the infernal fire of the conqueror's tyrannical descendants with their ultramodern weapons of steel, could prevent you from rising one day with your clenched fists scraping the skies to claim what is yours and what you are.

And you'd know as surely as you sense when you look out from the top of the cordillera that there is no greater beauty than what you see, that no matter how long it will take, the day will arrive when you will surely leap enraged like the mountain's condor to rip out the eyes of your oppressors, or when you will come close to them at the least expected hour as it was taught to you by the viper that crawls through your deserts, to poison the blood of your tormentors, to recover the land that was stolen from your ancestors. For the earth belongs to those who touch it lovingly with their breath and their daily sweat.

You will stand there on the top of the hill knowing better than anyone that this feeling of the earth is the only one that gave you strength even on the implacable dawn when our captors appeared five hundred years ago wrapped in the mist of the river;

when we first heard the thundering noise of the hooves of their mighty horses suddenly razing our placid valley, bearing those impudent riders with armor and lance, with their terrible spewing fire, with their shield and their cross; those creatures who turned out to be men like you but who, upon first seeing them, could not be differentiated from the beasts they mounted because you had never seen a man on a horse before; those bearded beings who roared in a strange language, whose skin was like the river's foam and who craved for gold the way we crave for water when on our long journey we thirst through the dusty deserts far away, the way we crave for salt when the meat of the hunt is about to be consumed, and as we will always crave for freedom.

Before the invaders arrived in our village, we gathered all the gold and all the treasures of our beloved gods and carried them to the top of the hill where we were born for generations, where a lake awaited us, where one need not be afraid of evil because two gods would be there to protect us, looking down, one through the lonely night and the other throughout the long day.

Those of us who climbed to the top of the mountain that day numbered over one thousand, counting the women and children. The old ones, the infants and the sick remained in the village. Silently, we cast all the possessions coveted by the white warrior into the deepest part of the lake. The gold and the engraved images studded with precious stones, sacred to us, sank rapidly in the deep and inaccessible shadow of the lake's bottom.

The sonorous echoes of the beasts were heard through the mountains. And then he appeared, wrapped in death's fury, scourging the valley with the frenzied gallop of his wild steed, he and his monstrous cavalcade, the ancient blasphemy of fierce conquerors on their livid lips and the bristling, crazed stampede suddenly exploded into a satanic thunderclap, leaving behind nothing but a trail of blood and ashes.

The following morning the huts, still in flames, stood like smoking torches on the immense, inflamed scar of the valley, crepitating toward the sky's throbbing sun. But neither the gold nor the gods' images were found; only a few scraps among the abandoned ruins in the rush of the exodus. The invaders carefully searched each hut before setting fire to it and, not finding anything they valued, their fury mounted until it became frenzy at the noon of the second day when they finally tore out a confession from one of the bleeding moribund tongues they tortured without compassion.

The conquerors marched up the hill in file, desecrating our holy ground for the first time, in search of the villagers and elusive gold, certain of finding both at the summit by the lake. But when they eagerly tumbled upon the top of the hill, a macabre feast of death confronted them suddenly, and a suffocating stench of putrefaction overcame them, forcing them to retreat, horrifying those untamed chargers when they beheld the million fluttering feathers of countless vultures clapping a diabolical multitude of wings, death's own ovation to the cowardly victor, flitting savagely in sinister clouds from corpse to corpse with red, festive claws and beaks from which torn bits of entrails still lingered in their tugged, avid and gluttonous disputation. Thousands of scavengers gulped down the decaying flesh of the villagers who had hanged each other and themselves from the mango trees bordering the placid lake where many of the drowned women and children floated aimlessly. And those who swayed from the trees had made sure their backs would be turned toward the path where they knew the enemy must pass, to express their disdain and rage, so that even in death their pride would not expire, looking toward the lofty mountains at the moment of entering eternity and now with mute and frozen stare fixed upon the distant horizons of their homeland.

The gold was lost in the fathomless bottom of the lake. And the conquerors felt invaded by a numbness toward the villagers in their attempt to deny what they beheld. For a few moments only, their inordinate zeal for gold lay dormant, until beginning the descent to camp, fleeing the nauseating stench and fearing a plague, they realized that a primitive people had preferred to die rather than live under their yoke. In the conquerors' retreat, the first they had suffered in all their campaigns in the New World—overpowering each time the flimsy arrows with their fire spewing machines—they felt cheated, thwarted in the face of death, and their numbness turned into disbelief. They wondered indignantly how these barbarous heathens dared to show such obstinate contempt, such subtle derision, such utter rejection as to die with their backs turned toward such noble conquerors.

Night extinguished the light of day and a twilight curtain of eviscerated figures rested, closely watched by satiated sentinels. And the vacuous eyes of the heavens, birds and the hanged villagers slowly closed upon the vivid image of each other as the curtain of bodies and tree branches, barely oscillated by the soft, tepid breeze, became dense, indistinguishable, as bone rubbed against bone, leaf against leaf, flesh against flesh, feather against feather.

The dark, hushed, enormous wing of night slowly engulfed life and death, while the immortal dream of freedom rolled on among the stars as it had happened since the world began.

When dawn came, the soldiers attended Mass in the valley at the burial of two of the victors who had died—one from malaria and the other from an old wound—while the surviving villagers, mostly the elderly, the sick and lame, forlorn and burdened with the chains of a slavery they had never carried before, watched from afar in grave bewilderment, invaded by a recent fear which for them was unknown.

Ora pro nobis.

"Pray for us," the conquerors muttered.

As the prayers were mechanically repeated, the image of the endless rows of swarthy, half torn bodies hanging from the branches of the ghastly trees, with clusters of scavengers tearing out and gorging the putrid flesh, and the spectacle of the floating bodies of women and children upon the waters remained with the conquerors. Years later, after they had returned to their own country, Mother Spain, the scene at the mountain lake was the image they recalled with greatest frequency and the memory which portrayed the indelible impression of this green continent of their conquest for the rest of their lives. Their senses dulled as they prayed, they vaguely knew that it was not possible to speak of pity or love toward their comrades in arms, these two men who came to die in this valley of the new world they were conquering at all costs in God's name and for the honor and glory of their king. Now, with the scene of horror still so fresh, they could think of nothing else. Without sufficient margin in their thoughts to chase away the morbid recollections, they were unable to form even a small space for a refreshing or consoling thought. Kneeling in this savage land, it was strange how one could share with another soldier all the years of homeless hardship and fatigue, the exultation of a hundred battles, and yet feel so detached at the hour of his burial. Like an automaton, one could only repeat old words learned during childhood—*Dominus vobiscum*—and kneel again at the sound of the bell, smelling the strong odor of incense. And they looked away from the cross with the Christ stretched upon it, yet now and again surreptitiously peered toward the hill, toward the lake and the trees, without quite knowing why.

Nunc et in hora mortis nostre, amen.

Yes. Now and in the hour of our death.

SECOND PART

III
THE TRIUMPH

ALMOST FIVE CENTURIES HAVE PASSED AND WHAT happened on that day of flames is lost like a leaf in the storm of oblivion. The books of history do not relate the true events because they were written to praise the invaders. Only in the old ballads of the natives and in the stories transformed into legends by the fireside are found the details.

Five hundred years and twenty-five generations of men and women came and went, disappearing forever. But at dawn the sun still weaves the same golden thread through the fringes of the cordilleras.

Now, when the last vestiges of the night are dispersed, the silhouettes of churches built by the conquerors on the top of the hills are looked upon with reverence. The ancient gods were replaced long ago and the bells toll now a new message whose echoes resonate through the canyons.

A wistful and quiet sentiment, like a solitary soft breeze that caresses, is part of the landscape. But the darkness will lift completely and the light of the new dawn will embrace us with the rich promise of morning rising freely in the heavens. This is the hour before dawn, when the fog begins to dissipate, when the warmth of the new day is anxiously expected. Here, as it often happens in the provinces, all paths lead to the plateau at the summit where the village grew along the ridge of the mountain by a long and narrow street leading to the plaza and to the steps of the church's atrium.

Those who come to the village for the weekly fair on Sundays begin the trip in darkness, carrying merchandise that weighs more than the carriers, who must walk at times over five leagues. Here and there an Indian chewing coca leaves to lessen hunger and retain strength, carries a load of mantillas, blankets, *ruanas,* necklaces and rings, his ancestral artifacts. But the majority bring vegetables and fruits, restless chickens inside crates or hanging by their feet from a stick, bread, or the small products of their home labor, of their manual work, in enormous baskets or barrels on their backs, tied with ropes or leather straps around their foreheads.

The figures walk bent, curved, burdened by the heavy weights, climbing firmly along the steep hillside. They walk in single file because the path is narrow, until they arrive at the outskirts of the village where the path slowly changes into a stony street. They move silently, knowing that in a few hours there will be rest; and that thought gives them strength to continue the painful march.

Often, the children are left behind to struggle with their loads, readjusting the weight so it will not hurt, learning during the course of each trip how to carry greater loads in less time and with less effort. Those who are too small to walk are carried on the backs of their mothers or older brothers or sisters. Sometimes there is a beast of burden among them, a little mule or an overloaded horse, constrained and worn out, moving hurriedly and without protest, eyes bulging, with a dull look staring at the path, walking precisely and rhythmically with the brute certainty of a habit acquired in a thousand similar trips, blind to the presence of the dangerous depths that open from time to time on both sides of the trail, depths waiting patiently for some careless victim to step falsely and fall into the obscure precipice where the final scream vanishes, unheard by anyone.

No one wants to stop to rest in the midst of the climb for fear of losing the momentum required to reach the top. But when one of the small ones begins to cry, a child lingering behind and who now feels weak, the elders stop, turning around to give words of encouragement:

"We're almost there boy, another little hill and we'll arrive!"

And if the child continues disheartened and weak in his struggle:

"Hurry up. If we don't arrive before dawn the souls from purgatory will chase us on the way down."

And that is the threat they most fear, because the return trip, the way back down the steep path, is always a happy occasion, an easy stroll without the overwhelming loads.

It is true that even on the way down some provisions must be carried but the agonizing weights are absent, replaced by a merry little bag filled with coins tied to the neck and which, hidden under the *ruana*, bounces upon the chest with each step, keeping pace with heartbeats.

On the other side of the mountain, not far from the village, a man, his woman and their child moved slowly toward the lofty mountaintop with the family's articles for the market. The man carried a great quantity of clay pots of various sizes in a wooden crate—plates for cooking, flower pots, all packed in such a way that not an inch was lost. The pots were packed in rows: small pots inside bigger ones, all wrapped among blankets and mantillas so friction would not break the delicate objects. These vessels were the product of the entire family's labor which included the elderly parents who could no longer make the trip and who remained in the hut where they lived with other relatives on a parcel of rented earth by the hillsides of the mountain next to the narrow valley.

The man rested on only two occasions during the long trip. His family knew the path by heart, each step, each stone along the way.

When he heard the groaning from his son a great distance behind him, it indicated that it was impossible for the child to continue walking and the man stopped by the side of a huge stone and leaned the load against it with extreme care so nothing would fracture. He slowly slid his back away from the load to see if the pack would stay on the rock, moving his head outside the leather strap which served as a harness. He did not let go entirely until he was sure the load would not be overturned by the wind. Finally he released the pack with great care when it rested firmly on the hillside.

His woman, a few steps behind, upon seeing her man getting ready to unload his burden, moved close to help and waited while he slowly began to move his head out of the leather harness that imprisoned him. She stood next to her mate while he untied the straps.

Now that he felt free, he extended his arms toward the sky feeling the cold wind soothing the pain of his sweaty back, his eyes squinting toward the sun which was about to be born. His face was filled with heavy drops of sweat and he wiped it with the wet rag his wife carried around her shoulders after she handed it to him. Then he helped his woman get rid of the weight that burdened her and dried her face tenderly while he looked in her black and tired eyes.

Once used, he returned the rag and moved a few steps away from her toward the edge of the precipice that opened up before his feet. Looking down into the depth of the abyss, he observed the delicate stream of his urine while it disappeared in the fog, a fine golden thread that descended toward the dark void below, unburdening himself with short and intermittent spasms of his whole body and with soft grunts of pleasure.

The child stopped crying and joined them, taking off his load also and coming to sit next to his mother.

There they rested for a short time to appease their weariness but still anxiously knowing that they must hurry to the market if they wished to find a good place, preferably by the shadow of one of the trees in the plaza next to the steps leading up to the church where the majority of buyers congregated.

If they could sell everything at good prices, some of the coins would surely find their way to the secret place under the hut, where they would be added to those already buried. Someday, perhaps, they would have enough to try their luck in the great city where, according to everything they had heard in many trips to the village, life extended the promise of permanent work in one of the many factories if one was fortunate.

The shadows cleared and the air promised a cloudless and warm day. They stood up and the man placed a hand upon the shoulder of the little one, firmly but with tenderness, looking directly into his eyes.

"Today you will be our guide. Show us the path toward the marketplace." That is what he spoke, but he said much more with his eyes and the child understood and smiled proudly.

"All right, let's go," said the man as though he were speaking to himself, rearranging the basket on his son's back and helping him take the first few steps.

"Let's climb the last hill," he added.

And now that the man was ready to struggle again with his own load, he looked at it with anger because it appeared to be stubbornly rooted, as though the overwhelming pack were part of the unmovable rock.

He readjusted the leather strap around the enormous weight and huddled up to the load like a dwarf, tightening the strap onto his sore forehead. Then he placed a knee on the ground breathing deeply, filling his lungs avidly and repeatedly, getting ready for the stretch; and he scraped a fistful of earth to give himself courage and to dry his hands, so the strap would not slip. By making a sustained and gradually increasing effort, he began to move his head forward, kept immobile by the strong strap. Trembling, he gradually began to shift the enormous weight upon himself with great care not to lose the delicate balance, knowing he would have to do it well the first time. Finally, the whole weight was ripped off the rock and remained flattened against his back with all its crushing volume.

The man shook himself to move the oppressive load, changing its position a trifle in order to get a better hold. The pack had not remained on the precise place where he could carry it, the exact spots he wanted it to press on his back, and from his mouth came a groan while he stretched himself.

For a moment he stood there among the towering majesty of his land and he felt strong, invincible, while his woman and child looked at him without knowing yet for certain whether he would be able to take the first step. He gazed at the horizon and filled his lungs again with that fresh air of the mountain. He moved his feet slowly till they were planted in the direction of the path they must follow. But when he tried to walk, his legs shook involuntarily in spasmodic convulsions until he was able to take command and control them, remaining upright upon the path.

He could not speak now that his jaws were tightly closed but he could emit a guttural and prolonged sound while he let out the air from his lungs. And upon filling them again, that groan which began from agony finished in a jubilant roar of defiance, well understood by his woman and son and which signified that he could control the load alone and had again triumphed. He began then to walk slowly but firmly.

This was how they made their last effort: the child walking before his parents, establishing the rhythm of the march with pride, feeling a new importance because this was the first time he guided the way toward the market, intent on moving as fast as his small and untrained legs would take him, no longer complaining but determined to demonstrate that he could be as strong and as indomitable as his father; the man, a few steps behind, breathing deeply and methodically, groaning once in a while, keeping his mandible tightly pressed in his monstrous battle against the wearing and inert adversary while he attempted to give courage to his son, knowing now that whatever would happen in life this boy of his would never surrender; and the woman, moving with certainty in the rear guard, concentrated on her private struggle but glancing at times toward her man and son to make sure they continued triumphant, and confident that she could walk like this with them until the end of the world, wherever they would take her.

And in this manner they walked, the three of them, toward the outskirts of the village on that market day while in the horizon, the sun, that god they had almost forgotten, leaped sovereign from the mountains toward the sky of the new dawn, exuberant and ripe.

IV
THE RECRUIT

IN THE VILLAGE EVERYONE KNEW HIM.

One day he disappeared when a patrol came to induct unwary peasants into the army. He had met the patrol at the outskirts of town and they took him even though he told them he was his elderly parents' only means of support; that without him they would be abandoned, at the mercy of old age. But the soldiers took him no matter what he said. His protests were not heard. When the army came to recruit, nothing could save the peasants or the Indians from being inducted against their will.

He was to walk for two days with his hands tied behind his back and a rope around his neck fastened to the saddle of a mule. In the mountains, before arriving in the city where the army barracks were located, he tried to escape but they chased him and after a few hours captured and beat him so severely that he lost his eight front teeth and was almost blinded by the kicking they inflicted upon his face. He was unable to open his purple and swollen eyes for a week. On the third day they took off the handcuffs and gave him a piece of hard bread and a bowl full of sweetened water. For three weeks they left him lying in the darkness of the prison cell without any medical services in spite of his prolonged moaning. They promised to kill him as a traitor of his homeland if he ever tried to escape again.

He served four years in the army and at the end of his enlistment they allowed him to return to his village to pick up the thread of his life. Toothless as they left him, with several deep scars on his face, his skin weather-beaten by the scorching sun of entire months spent outdoors, he was transformed drastically. But the external changes were slight compared to those suffered by his character: the tortures of his escape and of the prison cell, the constant humiliation and the abuses by his superiors, the blind obedience he had to keep night and day and the interminable months of guard duty, had turned him into a mistrusting and suspicious man who frequently blinked as though frightened and persecuted. There were other reasons why his metamorphosis had been so complete, reasons he tried to forget, events that haunted his nightmares. He had changed in body and in spirit in such a thorough way that now, when he returned to his village, no one recognized him. It isn't that he had aged twenty years in four; he was unrecognizable. He had changed totally.

As the bus that brought him from the city on the last leg of his return approached the village and he began to see the familiar places of his childhood, a profound anxiety overtook him. Suddenly, as the bus entered the village, he got off without waiting for the vehicle to stop, as he had skillfully done during his adolescence. He sat down to watch those who came to the marketplace, looking at the passersby with his mouth wide open. No one recognized him. He did not dare speak to his acquaintances who now looked upon him with a certain amazement, as though they were in the presence of a ghost, a phantom from long ago who made them feel slightly uneasy for some reason beyond their awareness. They looked upon him inquisitively, feeling there was something familiar about him, but when they saw how disfigured he was plus his military shirt, they avoided him, retreating, deflecting their gaze awkwardly, almost certain they didn't know him. And he behaved in a strange way toward them as well: if someone stopped to look at him, he withdrew and looked in the opposite direction, fearful that they would recognize him. When they didn't look at him, he came close to see if they would recognize him. He didn't know whether he wanted to be recognized or not.

Slowly, he began to walk the length of the main street that would carry him across the village toward the hut that had been his home for the first seventeen years of his life, looking with fascination at all the streets and houses that were so well known to him, cautiously coming close to the various groups in front of the taverns and in the central park, trying to listen to conversations without entering them.

He thought of asking about his parents, but the anxiety he felt did not permit him to do so. He finally chose to come near the groups without speaking, to find out whatever he could about the last four years of life in the village. After all, he was not in any hurry and he could give himself enough time. He had nothing else to do. This freedom also caused him to feel oppressed. And he realized, with a certain sadness he could not decipher, that he was not only pretending to be a stranger but, after all his suffering and his prolonged absence, he was a stranger among his old neighbors.

He felt as though he had never lived in this little village he knew so well, as though he had never listened to the *bambucos* of the sugar mills that were played by the bohemian guitars of the tillers with pouch and poncho, and never had known the peaceful afternoons after the laborious working days in the furrows of their mountains.

He thought he might be able to hear a reference to the happenings of four years before and in that way, without asking for it directly, be able to gather the fragments of his uprooted life and perhaps feel again as he had before; be able to recover what he had lost.

He felt a remote melancholy—as though it were not his own sadness but that of the entire village—which momentarily and without apparent reason made him think of the resounding echoes of an ancient ax his father had used many years before in the forests of the hillsides. A vague sadness he was unable to understand or express in words, but which hindered him like a knot in his heart, or a foggy veil before his eyes overtook him. Perhaps it was more like a barrier inside his being which imprisoned him and led him toward a path he did not wish to follow.

Little by little he pieced together the bits of conversations he overheard, the fragmented words flowing inevitably in mournful murmurs, barely reaching his ears, but which he captured in their full significance: fear of poverty and of abuse from the authorities had replaced the old ways; the army was bent on subduing them under any pretext; the overwhelming increment in the cost of daily life transformed agrarian labor into a heartless and backbreaking toil which was more akin to slavery than to honest work and which now was a continuous affront to the sentiment of dignity that had always been an inextricable part of their existence. The villagers had lost the pride with which, even during very difficult times, they had used to overcome disappointment and adversity.

Everywhere he heard the same story, the same complaints. And he found everywhere the desire to escape, to leave the village in search of better fortune, to abandon everything behind and forget, and to take the road toward the industrial centers in the crowded cities where they might be able to preserve a shred of dignity in the midst of the anonymity of the crowd, away from prying eyes. Much to his sorrow, instead of the peaceful days of his childhood, he found only anguish.

Each time he captured a piece of some conversation, the knot he felt in his heart tightened, his eyes welled tears and the barrier inside his being cornered him with increasing power until he again felt like a prisoner, worse than he had felt during his years in the army. After all, this was his village and here he had come to pick up the thread of his life. Now that all these people were saying it was no longer worthwhile to continue living in the town, repeating here and there that life had become unbearable under the conditions of misery, he felt completely disappointed.

His anger was difficult to overcome and incited him to walk faster in the direction of the hut where he had lived for so many years. He walked through familiar streets that led him to the other side of the village. Every stone of the road seemed like a living memory from the past. He moved cautiously at first, as though an enemy might be present, even though the streets were almost deserted.

As he moved away from the center of the village, one or another house still exhibited the violent marks of plunder and at times the ruins. The mute rubbish screamed of nights in flames and of the death of innocents, with only the cruel wreckage as witness. He accelerated his step, but upon coming closer to the place where long ago he had dreamed of becoming a man, an unutterable knowledge was hurriedly formulated in his thought, and the certainty that he would never see his parents again began to torment him.

He thought of the little hut with the two rooms, so fragile and so poorly furnished that its existence could have been undone in a matter of minutes and all vestiges of those who had lived there and the objects used by his ancestors erased during a short storm of violence, in a momentary shaking of agony followed by a sepulchral silence. He knew well that shaking and that silence. A chill overwhelmed him as he began to feel a furious rush of memories which he tried vainly to put out of his mind by moving his head brusquely as if wishing to tear out of his brain the images of cruelty and violence of the last four years.

When at last he arrived at the place where he should have found that intimate reality of his childhood, the small structure that could perhaps still have saved his life, he found, instead of the hut, nothing more than tall grass. He realized inescapably that his ominous premonition was a fatal arrow that had not missed its mark. He closed his eyes when he saw the grass was already taller than himself on the piece of land where his home should have been. He bent down fearfully and began to search among the grassroots until he found pieces of scorched wood. And as he desperately unearthed the burnt fragments already half-rotted and corroded by time and worms, the debris of what had been the dwelling of his childhood, those memories of his four years in the regiment which he had tried in vain to exorcise from his mind—the experiences which had truly transformed his life more than the beating he had suffered—finally invaded him, taking hold of him completely.

Yes, he too had done damage equal to the one he now witnessed. He had followed orders to kill the innocents, the children of muleteers and peasants; to harm other Indians, calling them bandits or *guerrillas* or communists, as was the custom to justify their slaughter, when in reality they were the opponents of the regime defended by the uniformed mob, hidden in the homes of the townsfolk who risked their lives protecting them, and often children who had nothing to do with this world of wild adults. He too had been an accomplice in the national fratricide committed in the provinces. He was part of the constant worry that propelled the people from the countryside to find refuge in the cities.

In the beginning of his military service, after the torment by his superiors ended, he felt forced, but later he participated in the campaigns without repugnance, without even thinking, as if it were an everyday happening; taking jubilantly of the scarce booty of others' wealth which, after all, was the only payment he received, feeling the imponderable satisfaction during the killing as he realized for the first time that others were afraid of him. And he remembered the pride he felt after so much humiliation and deprivation when they gave him the uniform in which he would become the living incarnation of the dread he would inspire and which, for a poor man like himself, had been the only way to win a crumb of respect and importance among men.

Here, in his village, he continued scraping the ground with ever-increasing eagerness which was transformed into vehemence when he found a piece of burnt stick that had been half buried in the ground's decay and which finally he recognized as one of the legs of the old family bed, the one used by his ancestors, where his parents had conceived him and where he was born, where they had protected him from the cold with their warm bodies during the winter nights of his childhood, where his parents had slept together through the twenty thousand nights of their lives before they were taken by surprise and annihilated. But just as he realized what he held in his hand, he flung that piece of wood from his past with loathing, vomiting a sour and thick substance which tasted like salt and rotten blood and seemed to come out in uncontrollable waves more from the depth of his soul than from the overwrought sinuosities of his intestines. In this manner, kneeling there, he sensed a cowardice about himself greater than any feeling he had ever experienced in his entire life, knowing that he too had inflicted comparable pain, that his parents had died in one of the thousand ways that his own tormentors had taught him to kill during the four years of service to his homeland.

He detached his body from the refuse of his prior home and began to run, thinking he did not wish to know the details of what had occurred, disposed now not to approach those who had been his neighbors.

He wished to live and die at the same time and did not know how to do one or the other. He didn't know where to go nor how to begin or end, feeling the necessity to survive like the animal whose biological destiny was to continue breathing so that his own species among the other animals of the planet would not become extinguished. A species that would remain only to be discovered in a thousand million years by some superior investigator who would instantly recognize him as a member of a strange breed called *Homo sapiens*. A breed that had not been able to adapt itself or to develop appropriately because of a lethal genetic factor of willful destructiveness in its chromosomatic mutation that inescapably deflected him from his rightful destiny and which was passed on from generation to generation until his whole tribe was dragged toward its inexorable doom. And, at the same time, he struggled with the unstoppable wish to die so he would not have the human opportunity to resolve the hatred that gnawed inside him and feel the sublime love that could always transform him into a being exquisitely vulnerable and sensitive to the smallest depredation.

In the midst of this unutterable conflict his steps took him to the church, behind which was the cemetery. His steps were mechanical and automatic, just as they had carried him so many times during the years of his childhood and as he had been taught to march in the regiment. He thought about seeing if his parents were buried there and in this way at least bring a closure to that part of his life. He buttoned up the collar of his military shirt. His almost martial step made him remember the many marches toward distant and defenseless villages with a rifle on his shoulder. And he felt as though he were again under the orders of a superior; and that act, being so akin to obedience brought him a certain calmness, making him feel like he didn't have to continue thinking about impossible decisions which wore him out.

Once he arrived at the cemetery behind the church, he walked with precision toward the high vaults where the tombs of the poor were marked on the lime walls. The number of the dead had grown lately. He examined in silence the names of hundreds of people he had known, people who had been his friends. Half the world he had loved was now cloistered in these mute walls with their interminable rows of tombs.

At last, his inquisitive glance stumbled upon the names of his parents, engraved on the highest row. They had received at least holy burial in exchange, most likely, for the small parcel of land no one had claimed, a piece of dirt that would be added to the ever-increasing possessions of the Church. One was next to the other, the same date of expiration on both tombs. And knowing now with certainty the kind of death that must have seized them at the same hour, he suspected that those burned and gnawed fragments which scarcely remained of the fragile memories of his childhood would be transformed in a few instants into ashes which the most ephemeral breeze would sweep toward the inaccessible places of his being where they would remain buried and forgotten like a happy dream that was violently interrupted during the first dawn of his life when memories were still impossible. Only for an instant did he fix his eyes upon those parental names which already appeared alien and which had not left any other trail upon the earth, and on the engraved date which would remain anonymously suspended in the wall as an insignificant fragment in the immensity of time.

Those who saw him come out of the cemetery in front of the church were aghast as they beheld him because he walked as though he were bewitched, as though he moved under the scrutiny of some harsh general reviewing his troops. His eyes were fixed in the distance and he was deaf to every stimulus except for that interior purpose which obeyed an invisible force propelling him like a puppet.

It was then, the moment he left behind that row of tombs, when everything tying him to the village disappeared, when he felt the sudden arrival of a terrifying emptiness inside his head, an emptiness which separated him from everything real he had known.

The village was converted into ice and glass, with streets and houses that were square, rectangular, sharp-pointed, parallel, rectilinear; where all the forms straightened out, becoming perpendicular, triangular and remained inflexible, unbending, without any hint of roundness; where colors vanished and the whole universe was reduced to the variations between black and white.

Everything froze and became slippery like a mirror reflecting itself; inhuman and distant. The village was a desert without sands; glossy, rigid. The trees remained static, the wind stopped blowing, nothing seemed to move although men walked and children and dogs ran as they had always done, but now they remained suspended without reaching their goal, like in an interminable nightmare.

He didn't look at anyone but sensed that all the people were objects who had also lost one of their dimensions. What they lacked now was depth: they were long and broad, but the third dimension had disappeared. Their bodies were made of plaster, of clay, of lime. Everything was about to break and crumble.

From the trees, insipid fruits were hanging. In the sky, the clouds had turned into parallel rivers of white blood; puddles of gray blood stagnated, and seas of black blood were agitated.

Everything was petrified in what to him became the mirage of the village. He stood in the middle of the park in front of the church in a posture of military attention, as though he were waiting for a superior to put him at ease but unable to do so by himself. The whole village was perplexed by his unusual conduct. He remained in that position of statue the rest of that day and the whole night, without eating, without attending to his physical needs until dawn, when the villagers ran terrified, fleeing from the platoon of soldiers who had entered the town again to recruit whomever they could catch. As was their custom among the unwary peasants, they arrived to gather as many helpless Indians and poor people as possible.

The old men, the women and children who did not need to escape said that when the soldiers saw him standing in the middle of the park in his rigid posture and approached him, he greeted them in perfect martial form with an impeccable military salute, in accordance with the best possible training, and they say he was heard to utter only three laconic words, firmly enunciated, convincing, the only words he had uttered during his entire stay in the village: “I will obey!” He then followed the leaders voluntarily, helping them in their tasks as if he had always been a soldier and would remain one all his life.

The last time they saw him he was lost in the ranks of the uniformed army which, with their many new recruits, youngsters, peasants and Indians from the countryside who walked with ropes tied to their necks and attached to the saddle of a mule, was headed toward the army headquarters in the outskirts of the city.

V
THE DUEL

STAND ON TOP OF THE CORDILLERA, AND, IF THIS IS the place you spent your youth, you will hear the soft murmur of the wind speak in the accents of freedom. And if your hand touches the earth, the heart within your breast will know that this earth is yours.

But if you walk down the stony paths toward the river, you will know that man's inexorable steps have left deep furrows upon the splendid valley. Look around and you will see the many giant bridges under which the river moves forever, its strength already tamed, its power held; and watch the railroad along its shores taking man's ageless and agonizing toil toward the horizon and beyond. Look how the hundred factory chimneys point toward the sky. Tall buildings crowd the center of the valley, huddled against the cathedral, hunchbacked colossus whose somber, waxy arms hover mutely over the city, its extended fingers scraping the clouds.

Now you are far from the sea and the burning desert. You cannot hear the roaring turbulence of swollen waters nor the screaming sands, and neither ice nor snow will touch you.

Here, in this city you shall know poverty in your mother's arms. You shall look up at the sky and see her face, and she will sing a song in your ears, your own cradle song which you will repeat with the first words of your mouth, taught by the conquerors to your ancestors long ago. The song speaks of angels like yourself and of the life you will enjoy some day long after the scorpion will have made his nest within the socket of your eye. The song speaks of a home, celestial and free from care or rent or mortgage. It will not be made of manure or tin cans like your home on the hills of this world but of sweet, eternal love. Neither will it stand upon a piece of ground sold in small parcels on a twenty-year loan to those fortunate enough to escape the crowded tin slums, but in Heaven, where all things are possible and where you will see the face of God.

And you will live happily ever after.

Oh, eternal love, you will not be absent after the tarantula weaves her lugubrious dwelling place in our withered hair! For ours will be the kingdom of heaven where we shall be comforted and filled. And we shall inherit the earth, obtain mercy, and sit by the right hand of God. We shall be called the children of God if we bury our wrath and forget the five hundred desolate years of our captivity. And we shall finally rest in the House of the Lord into all infinity if we keep our hearts pure while the cuckolds force our sisters to sell their bodies in the bright palaces of lust, if we hunger and thirst after righteousness while they keep us out of the universities and, above all, if we obey and submit like nice little lambs.

But in the meantime, while the worm eagerly awaits our flesh, let the meekest and the hungriest among us beg for a piece of cardboard and a few yards of wire from the warehouses of the mighty; let him burrow and scrape into the dung heaps and the fortresses of garbage in the outskirts of the great industrial city and, with his wife and joyful children, drag like crabs the scraps of discarded tin plates; fill their sacks with tin cans that only recently stored delicious foods they will never taste, whose remnants may yet be gulped in shame, and carry the glorious loot across the streets and fields and up the craggy peaks of the hills where the gallantry and generosity of the city fathers will allow him and a million others to carve out of the ground with his machete a small place to rest his head and build his own room of tin walls, tin roof, cardboard beds and newspaper mattresses for a very reasonable fee for the entire family.

He will build his room upon a high place overlooking the city, and if he can spare a few coins for bribery they will allow him to live near a creek where his pregnant wife will not have to work more than a few hours daily hauling water.

He will rise with the first sign of dawn and make his way down the teeming hillside among the other tin and cardboard rooms. And if he is to have good fortune, it will not be until late at night when he will return each day, exhausted and consumed from the work at the factory, where his powerful back will have carried enough bales of cotton to clothe him and his ancestors for five centuries.

But now let him drag his loot quickly through the prying streets, for greedy eyes haunt him and a man with a more bitter life than his, a larger family of starved children, a man even more battered by the whiplash than himself, more poisoned, already stalks and seeks him out as his own prey. With cunning eyes, panting with a furious heart, the gleaming of his unsheathed machete concealed under his ragged poncho, he waits for his victim around the deserted corner of a lonely street.

The holiday hangs by its zenith and fifty more years of sunshine stretch out before him, but he throws it all into the vortex and gambles everything against nothing. Is it madness that hurls him on, suddenly screaming curses across the suffocating street against this unsuspecting adversary? Or does he want to steal what the man has gathered?

A mighty roar that echoes down the empty streets reverberates, shrieking from the throat of the despoiler. His eyes bulge and the dark veins of his thick throat wildly throb with each stroke of his desperate heart. His left hand whirls the poncho, wrapping it around the taut muscles of his arm to shield his naked chest with rags, while his right hand firmly clutches the lethal weapon. Sensing the advantage of surprise he leaps confidently, pointing the hissing blade straight up as far as his arm can reach toward the sky for the added power the arm will need when it is brought down upon the dark, mute face of the victim, who turns and stares dumbly at the gaping mouth of his attacker only for as long as it takes the sun's reflection on the raised weapon to strike his eye and warn him of the descending danger.

And as men have always desperately attempted to interpose anything, no matter how flimsy or ephemeral, between themselves and their executioners, to gain, even in the gullet of disaster, another precious instant of prolonged existence, he placed one of the rusted pieces of tin—what was to become a part of his family's shelter in the turpitude of the hills—between himself and the shattering blade, brought down so mightily that the tin plate was impaled and the point of the blade trembled for an instant inside the prominent cheek of the victim, eliciting a torrent of blood and desperate, agonized screams from those for whom the wounded man had toiled: his wife who stood bewildered, unable to believe what was happening, feeling heavy with the weight of metal and pregnancy, and her small and startled children clinging to her faded skirt and dragging the sackfuls of tin cans, dissonantly clanging in the midst of the wailing street.

In spite of the vehement efforts of the attacker to maintain his initial advantage with a repeated avalanche of furious blows with the machete, the bleeding victim, now rolling in the dust, now leaping, now backing against a cement wall that served as a springboard to avoid the thousand eager flames brought near the flesh by the cutting edge, finally gained time through the momentum of his few furious steps to unsheathe in frantic desperation the redeeming, vengeful machete he carried by his waist. Letting his persecutor feel the impact of steel upon steel, he smiled savagely, with a diabolical grin and spat blood on his face, screaming the ancient cry of anticipated victory which had always given the enemy pause, a moment to restore shrewdness and feel the sweet passage of time, to scheme the forthcoming mortal blows of the combat.

He began filling his lungs with air, avidly breathing like a man escaped from a whirlpool, laughing to cover up his panic, waving his machete with his right hand, his own poncho tightly wrapped around his left arm for shield, keeping his adversary at a distance, commanding his wife and children to get off the street, now cursing in a shrill, mocking voice to provoke impulsive attack, scratching the dirt with his toes and kicking dust toward the encircling enemy who, taken aback, was recovering and going through similar motions.

Now both are standing a few paces apart, scurrying sideways, waving the machetes in wide circles and taunting each other, rhythmically thrusting their pelvises forward while reaching down with all five fingers of the left hand and grabbing, tugging, shaking at each other their concealed and bulging sex organs under the thin drill pants, screaming curses back and forth, now moving their arms like the wings of fighting cocks and crowing wildly:

"Hijuepuuuuuuta! Son of a biiiiiiitch!"

The wounded man's dribble of blood from his cheek was held back by a handful of dust he picked up in the street and pressed into the gash. His wife was on her knees, the loot of tin sheets and cardboards scattered on the street, with the children huddled against her. She raised her arms and wailed the prayer of the valley.

"Don't let them kill my man! Blessed God, don't take away my man!"

A few stray, cadaverous dogs, who chanced to hear the clamor and wailing in the street, barked in the distant corner and ensued a jaded trot toward the commotion, hoping for some kind and generous spirit to toss them a bite of food.

"There goes your mother whore with the rest of the scabby dogs!"

"Watch out bastard! I'm gonna kill you! Heee, heeee, heeee, heeee!"

His laughter was forced and frightened although it conveyed a confidence that continued to keep his assailant at a distance. The two men studied each other's movements carefully, feigning to leap forward, laughing, and then again retreating.

An enormous blood bubble formed above his mustache as he laughed, a viscous, pale red, rotating bubble with bits of dust and mucous. It became larger until it reached down into his mouth and up toward his eyes. Then it burst as suddenly as it had formed, startling him and splattering a few speck of blood over one side of his face and into his glistening, black eye. He rubbed himself with the poncho, blinking. But in that instant he felt again the thousand suns burn his flesh and heard the strange wailing of his wife's voice and the barking of the dogs. The blade's point had penetrated through the shielded arm and he felt a dull ache in his elbow. His contender was already at a safe distance laughing and making teasing gestures like a rooster. When he noted that he already had two wounds bleeding profusely and perceived how the other man remained completely unhurt, he was infuriated and instead of retreating, he attacked savagely. He must cut into his enemy's flesh, feel its soft resistance and sense the impasse of the bone. He thought of killing him and tearing his body into bits with the machete.

The fury of incessantly screamed insults, shrill laughter, the clashing of blade against steel and cement, the terrified wailing of the prostrate woman and her children, and the mocking bark of the pack of dogs filled the street. A few of the shutters nearby opened and people began coming out of the houses and running down the street in their Sunday best. A great cry, raised by a hundred voices old and young, was added to the din and clamor of the battle, proclaiming the wild news with no intention of concealing the inward joy felt at announcing the great and free spectacle of two men engaged in a bitter struggle of life and death.

"Pelea! Pelea! Fight! Fight! Over here, with machetes! Yeeeeheeee! *Pelea!"*

In a few moments a great circle was formed, allowing a respectable distance between the fighters. And the more they screamed the more people arrived from adjacent neighborhoods until the street was filled. The sea of spectators flowing into the crowded street began to take positions on window ledges, balconies, tree branches, car tops and patio walls from where the observation and thorough enjoyment of the fight would be unimpaired.

So suddenly was the street invaded by the multitude that the two men had barely recovered from their last attempt to maul each other when they found themselves in a shifting, violent nightmare surrounded by these eager strangers. Though intent on following each other's movements they heard the shrill exclamations from the crowd: *"Matálo, matálo!* Kill him! Cut him up! *Cométela vivo!* Eat him alive! Let's see who's the real macho!"

The grinning men looked at each other, their faces twitching, the wounded one trying to save strength by letting his attacker move in circles around him.

"Cooooooooocureeeecoooo!
Cooooooooocuuuuuuuriiiiicooooo!"

When they resumed their attacks against each other, a wild surge of approval came from the crowd. The excitement spread fast and the circle around the fighters tightened so dangerously close that when the machetes traced their sideways-sweeping, lethal orbits, the crowd pushed back and then forward again in a tempestuous wave under which the wife and children of the wounded man and some of the weaker spectators were trampled.

The ocean swelled and the overwhelming tide finally closed the circle completely, tossing into its current the wounded fighter and heaving him on top of his assailant at the very moment when his blade was aimed at his enemy's exposed dark skin above the wrapped poncho, aiding his thrust, adding a new fury to his impetus. Then he knew that his foe, this attacker who had assaulted him so treacherously during his peaceful task, would forever bear the indelible marks of his vengeance.

He screamed victorious, and the peculiar, instantaneous memory of a beggar with an amputated arm, huddled by the gates of the cathedral, crossed his vision as he saw the arm unhinge, limbering, as he saw a red fountain splash the dust, as he heard his enemy's wailing voice. But no sooner had his joy become known to him, no sooner had the vision been dipped in crimson and vanished, when he felt a tingling sensation on his own left wrist and sensed the tide of his blood pulling on his whole body as he tumbled and saw an emptiness, a red gap, his own stump, and unretrievably beyond his reach, his open hand, lonely in the multitude as it had always been, begging on the dust among the trampling feet.

The crowd ebbed, murmuring, and for an instant he thought he saw his wife crawling out of the circle of men surrounding him, crowding toward the resting hand that still bled as though it had a life of its own. He never knew whether he had dreamed it or if it actually had happened to him in the spring of his childhood in the hills' slums, but it seemed to him that long ago he heard a woman, perhaps his own mother, pray in gratitude to God for a pound of fresh meat that had been given to them, and he remembered how his mother's tears had fallen on the meat and she had kissed it, sobbing. It all seemed so confusing and strange now because he thought he saw her again and heard her praying, sobbing as she had done so many years ago, kissing that piece of bloody meat that inexplicably had the shape of his own hand, rocking it against her breast like a baby and desperately lamenting:

"No, no, no, *Dios mío*, my God, no, you killed him God, my poor man's flesh. Why? Why? Why? I asked you for our daily bread and here it is. You let them kill my man. Thank you; oh, thank you, and bless you!"

He listened, entranced as he staggered, until he heard a deafening and heavy thud in his ear, accompanied by another flood of blood that spewed out of his face and heard the sharp sound of bells tolling destructively. He fell and knelt and the other man tumbled over as well and sat close to him on the ground, both of them in the same puddle of blood that was already mixing with the dirt, each still brandishing his machete and pounding with well aimed but decreasingly vigorous blows on the other's face and neck and chest, until they both collapsed. They lay on the ground looking up at the purple sky, now spasmodically jerking their weapons, each thinking the battle had been proudly won, feeling the other's dying breath amidst the wild cries of the multitude. They looked at each other for a moment as though up until that instant they had not even seen each other and it was then that the pride which had overwhelmed them vanished as suddenly as it had arrived. And they heard themselves whisper: *"Matáme, 'manito, matáme.* Kill me, little brother, kill me."

She who held a callused, begging hand in her own hands crawled with her children toward the side of their dead protector to restore it, placing it against the bleeding stump while the other man, unable to move any longer, rolled his eyes upward to look at her with a supreme intensity and wailed with almost as much fury as he had before, when the street had been empty and he had leaped across it with a purpose only dimly understood:

"Don't let the bastards make bandits and whores out of our children! You hear me, woman? You hear me?"

The woman looked at him with fear and repugnance, sobbing while she caressed the dusty and bloody chest of her dead man, without understanding the meaning of the words hurled at her, feeling that in his delirium he had confused her with another woman, perhaps his own wife.

It was then that her barefoot boy, the oldest of her children, silently tore the machete from the still grasping hand of his father and, with great effort, lifted the heavy, bloody weapon overhead with both hands, discharging it with all his strength between the dying eyes of his father's killer, giving free reign to his feverish vengeance.

The street slowly emptied; the whispering groups of shadows moved away from death. Some of those who had been too far away to see all the details of the fight, and a few latecomers, moved close for a while, loitering about, staring dumbly at the corpses and at the child who had just killed a man, while several policemen arrived and carried the nameless bodies into an ambulance, followed by the screams and cries of the woman and her children.

Tomorrow the mute graves will sink. Perhaps tomorrow the sky will lose its purple hue. Tomorrow, the vibrant hills will cast out onto the city two more widows and a dozen or so more orphans, new beggars turned loose in the city.

But in the meantime, the dogs will lick the crimson corners of the street with avid, thirsty tongues.

VI
THE BEGGARS

FROM THE WOMB OF THE TATTERED WOMAN, THE creature could not see the distant light of stars. And the rest, children of glances distorted by hunger, with stomachs emptied by the lingering night, were too sleepy and busy walking down the hill. The smallest one was carried by her mother, wrapped in a black mantilla that hung from the woman's back while one of her other children could barely walk with his uncertain steps, grasping desperately at the protecting skirt, crying with a forced and hoarse moan as though he had been crying this way from the hour of his birth.

To appease him the mother searched in a bag dangling around her neck and pulled out a piece of brown sugar loaf which she placed in his mouth. But in spite of the hunger he had and how much he liked the sweet treat, the movements of the mother were so brusque that she only was able to aggravate the desperation of the small one. Finally she gave up and let him continue moaning while he devoured the brown sugar. The other three boys walked by the side of the woman and moved downhill without her help among the ruinous shanties, huts and caves where the swarm of those who were forsaken lived.

Among the four—the mother and the three eldest boys—they pushed a single-wheeled pushcart that had been laboriously worked over to make it look like a primitive wheelbarrow, rusted and almost completely destroyed, on which another child covered with newspapers and dirty rags was lying down.

It was difficult to discern in the penumbra of dawn the true age of this small one. Even when the light of day, when the glory of the sun illuminated the valley in such a way that no longer could anything lend itself to be confused with some hallucinated vision, with an infernal mirage, the age of that child remained fathomless. For the time being he slept under the rags and his head moved from side to side, bobbing up and down, as though it were inert, marking the sudden beat of each turn of the irregular and shrill wheel.

Sometimes it seemed like a jolt of the wheelbarrow would heave him upon the clumps of earth mixed with humid clay where they slid, or upon the hostile stones of the road, or to finally come to rest upon some fragment of moss by the side of the dark path. In spite of the constant jolts, he continued sleeping innocently with the tired and profound sleep of those who have entrusted their lives to another's destiny. Sometimes he seemed ready to wake up, holding his breath for a long time and then moving one or another extremity in a vague gesture of self-protection as though trying to embrace himself. But soon, he'd stop moving and resume the heavy breathing with a thick groan.

This way they came down into the city where the streets were deserted, with the nocturnal silence still dangling from the last stars. But as they approached the central plaza where the majesty of the cathedral rose toward the sky forming an enormous silhouette against the dawn, the eager blossoming of a new day forced them to hurry.

Today was the first day of the carnival and many people would come to commemorate the founding of the city. Strangers would come from lands beyond the seas. The activities of this day would climax when the archbishop would take out of the cathedral upon his shoulders a large golden vessel containing holy water to bless the frolicking costumed dancers and the monument to heroes in the square in a public demonstration of gratitude to the memory of the two conquerors who died for the Christian faith nearly five hundred years ago.

If she could only obtain a good place next to the main portal of the cathedral, where everyone entering had to pass, good fortune would perhaps smile upon her and her starving children. She was glad when the first rays of the sun, indisputable god of the firmament, focused upon her family and the cart, knowing that it would illuminate cruelly each piece of rag they were forced to wear, all the ravages of tiredness revealed in the emaciated flesh, the ineluctable signs of hunger: that fierce adversary who tormented them.

It wasn't until later, when at last they settled next to the wide portal of the cathedral, ready to be seen by everyone coming in and going out, that upon the insistence of the mother, each of the little ones thrust out the hand enslaved by poverty to make the universal gesture of the beggar.

She then removed the dirty rags and the newspapers covering the creature in the wheelbarrow, to allow the solar light to reveal the dreadful spectacle now contorting in the reflexive movements of nerves and flesh and bones that shook without reason, appendices of impotent extremities which in their awkwardness mocked the human life that still seemed trapped and immutable in the anguished eyes of the being whose enormous hydrocephalic head occupied the greater portion of the wheelbarrow.

The child's head—appearing all the larger because the rest of his body was so thin—resembled a colossal stone carved out to look like an infant's face, a relic rescued from the debris of rudimentary vestiges of some primitive tribe that ceased to exist long ago.

"Small alms, *por el amor de Dios*, for the love of God," the little children called out in unison.

"*Por el amor de Dios,* to calm the hunger," they repeated.

They grouped themselves on both sides of the portal, forming two rows between which the devout early risers walked in order to enter the cathedral.

At the end of this corridor of begging children was the pushcart with the abnormal child with the fixed and desperate eyes twitching unconsciously. There he was, exhibited like the macabre painting in the gallery of horrors of some master maddened by his fury against an unjust society, next to the mother who once in a while cleaned the spittle oozing by the corners of his open mouth where already the tenacious flies of the new day had begun to prey.

She picked him up out of the cart and placed him on her lap as she sat against the brick wall of the magnificent structure because she knew that if she could exhibit wisely the monstrosity that wriggled there for everyone to see, now spread across her arms and bosom, she could create such a profound impression among the faithful that the image would grow in their vision and remain with them for the whole hour the Mass lasted. She hoped and prayed for their hearts to soften enough to reduce any resistance they might have to give alms, dislodging little by little the rancor they might hold feeling the intrusion of the needy ones who begged and of this incredible scene in a fresh morning which should be a delightful preamble for the joy of the carnival, at a time when they did not wish to know about the misfortune of others.

She abstained from looking at them as they filed by her through the portal because she knew they would notice more the monster she held if they thought no one was watching them, if they felt alone contemplating misery without witnesses, without the look of adults they could interpret as recrimination. She knew that the more they looked at him the more irresistibly the image would become recorded in their memories.

And she knew for certain that they would have to satisfy their morbid curiosity and keep looking at the deformities. For a moment, a surge of having a bit of power over the onlookers invaded her. Later, when they would leave, she would nail her anguished eyes upon them, accusatory and imploring at the same time, when she would have her opportunity to trap the elusive coins. While she waited, she listened to the noise of the nascent city down there in the plaza where the daily concerns of a life seemed to elapse in a world so different from her own, a life foreign to her experience, making her feel alien in her own land, like an unwelcome guest, as if none of the beauty there belonged to her, as though she had no right to participate in this life which after all was the only one she would have.

She looked at the people bedazzled, forgetting for a few minutes the mission occupying her, her position in this world, and remained absorbed noting the marvelous facility in the movements of those milling about far down in the plaza, seeing how they laughed with such ease, observing the manner in which they enjoyed the new day. But as she began to feel in her reverie a small bit of the exuberance that was present in the plaza, some fragment of the morning's energy surrounding her, she suddenly felt the sharp pain of hunger in her stomach and the jerking of her intestines stretching in an internal convulsion upon lacking anything to feed itself. Her stomach emitted a prolonged growl.

She realized once more that all these strangers were inaccessible, immune to her pain, as though their entire lives were concentrated only on festivities and monies to spend, as though everything were so easy that one would only have to think of this or that to possess it freely, throwing away money that ran in torrents from hand to hand, redeeming bills that always circulated outside of her reach and with which she could obtain food to save her whole family.

She heard again the groans of the little one and unwrapping the last bits of brown sugar from her bag, she apportioned what was left of the loaf among the children who surrounded her immediately to receive the sweet they avidly devoured as they returned to their begging posts.

She suspected that the kind of happiness unfolding around her would never be part of her family's life as long as they had to depend on charity or the laws made by the owners of the city, and that by just asking nicely they would never have the right to live a peaceful life without the continuous and overwhelming violence of this terrorizing poverty.

Her face hardened again and she turned it toward those inside, banishing the momentary dream, the hope, narrowing her eyes and adopting a rigid posture as if she were trying to disappear somewhere where she would not need food to survive.

The priest's voice from the pulpit reached her vaguely. "Place your children's future in the hands of heaven and you will be taken care of," he preached. She looked vacantly in his direction with a slight smile of doubt on her lips. She had heard the admonition ever since she could remember and had trusted to no avail. She moved her head from side to side and shrugged her shoulders, mumbling.

She always thought about receiving more than what they ever gave her. She remembered a day long ago when she was a child and her family was invited into the large house of a wealthy man who took pity on them. There, behind the high iron gates which protected the mansion, they ate amply until they were filled. They could even take a few bowlfuls of leavings for the next day. Now, she swallowed saliva.

After the Mass ended and all the people had left, the beggars moved to a shadier spot by the sidewall of the cathedral. After four hours of begging they still had not collected enough coins to calm their hunger and they were exhausted, with hardly enough vitality to extend their hands toward the hated giver.

As they received some alms, the mother would send the oldest of her children to buy food for the small ones, but so little could be purchased that it was impossible to feed all of them. As the hours passed the internal contortions occurred with greater frequency.

"Don't you dare spend those coins on foolishness, you hear me? It's to buy milk for the little sick one."

But when the ill child with the extraordinary head felt upon his lips the contact of a warm bottle and intuitively realized they were trying to feed him at last, he desperately began to choke with the milk. In his greedy desire to consume everything at once, before one of the others could take the bottle away from him—even though the mother was always defending the sick one—he began to vomit everything he had already consumed.

"He don' like milk '*amá*,'' said one of the children. And feeling he had the right to the bottle because his sick brother had failed to drink, he snatched it away before the rest of the contents would go to waste and ran away with it, sucking it, laughing while he drank the milk in great gulps, chased by two of his brothers and by his mother's scolding shouts.

They continued begging through the sweltering afternoon. Once in a while, the mother and the eldest of her sons wished to feed the sick one who kept trying to move his head but could barely do so, attempting to help himself like a wounded animal, blurting out with great effort some incomprehensible complaint. He ate with an uncommonly large covetousness but shortly after swallowing whatever they gave him, he vomited and moaned again.

The other children ran through the park after having eaten a few crumbs, competing with each other in searching the garbage cans where they found something to carry away like a trophy, but which in reality amounted only to a piece of discarded meat or a half rotted fruit, picking up cigarette butts which they finished smoking with deep puffs as though these too were food to sustain life.

They ran recklessly through the park interrupting conversations as they begged, making transient friendships with other children in the same condition.

Seeing a well-dressed elderly lady carrying a purse in an isolated place behind the cathedral, three of the brothers pushed her against the wall and snatched the purse from her, leaving the lady moaning painfully on the street. They searched the purse after disappearing around the corner, taking out its insignificant trinkets and a few small bank notes and coins which they kept gleefully, then threw away the empty purse into a hole of the sewage system below. When they returned to their mother they bragged, showing her the bills proudly. And they ran to the market and bought a great variety of all sorts of cheap food and fruits which they carried in a paper bag.

The mother suspected they had taken the money illicitly, not by begging, but asked nothing of them. Each member of the family except the sick one chose what to eat and did so until satiated, leaning against the discolored wall of the cathedral, forgetting the sick one who had lost all desire for food, burning with fever, self-absorbed in his own suffering.

Slowly it began to darken and the cold air of the mountains descended to the city. For warmth, the smallest children huddled next to their mother who sustained the sick one in her arms, covering herself with a few sheets of the day's news that now were old, while the three bigger ones, feeling a new sense of camaraderie through the violent theft they shared, settled in an embrace on a large piece of cardboard they placed on top of the iron grill of the sewage system through which escaped a fetid but warm subterranean air emanating from the entrails of the city. Trusting, they surrendered to sleep, the three urchins who had tasted the illusory and transient gratifications of delinquency, the three loitering little beggars whose contribution to the future was sealed, irrevocably determined by their short past. But upon awakening, those children of the dawn felt anew the first omens of the hunger of the new day, the familiar emptiness in the stomach that only food would soothe.

They began again to beg on that second day of the carnival as their mother had done even before the days of giving them birth.

She had tried to feed him when he awoke but the sick child did not show any interest and closed his mouth. Breathing had become difficult and he emitted a few hoarse sounds each time he inhaled, attracting greater attention. The coins today were filling the tin can faster. She held it out in her trembling hand, making the coins sound like a rattle even though it wasn't her purpose to make such a discordant sound. She seemed to be in a hurry looking eagerly at each person walking by her side. With the other hand she cleaned the feverish sweat from the child's face and swatted at the insatiable flies.

Several times she emptied the tin can and hid the coins. They give more during a carnival when they're feeling happy, she mumbled. The hiding of the coins was done surreptitiously, afraid that if they'd find out how well she was doing today they would stop giving to her. The coins were hidden in a bag that hung from her neck under the dirty mantilla, anxiously counting them first to make sure they were not inventions of her imagination. She stopped looking at the child in her arms and devoted all her attention to the coins and the people who began to surround her.

She knew exactly the moment when the child in her arms died.

The enormous head unhinged itself upon her dry breast. The coarse sound of his breathing remained suspended and he slowly exhaled a warm air that left his chest flat. Those eyes which had searched the skies of his homeland hardened. A viscous and pale cover blinded them forever.

But the mother pretended not to be aware and continued exhibiting him for days after the child ceased breathing, clutching the coins voraciously, thinking about the survival of her other children, until a putrid odor began to come out of that inert and cold body which she could no longer keep warm no matter how hard she tried.

Because the stench scared them and made them gag, the other children moved away frightened, leaving the mother alone with the child decomposing in her arms, surrounded by onlookers with handkerchiefs pressed against their noses.

THIRD PART

VII
THE DREAM

THE VALLEY TURNED EAGERLY TOWARD EVENING seeking the hill's fresh breezes when the sun declined. Shadows extended across the city.

Man rests, waits and dreams his secret wish, holding his woman in his strong arms, sensing the soft presence of his mate through the loving and pale night. In the vision of his dream he looks at all men with pride and joy, speaks with them freely, and neither fear, envy nor rage pursue him. His children grow healthy and protected, unharassed, and the ground where he was born will never be taken away because it belongs to him and all his brothers and sisters. In his dream he knows the earth is vast and other valleys, other forests and mountains await the seed of his descendants. He will build the safe city where all the people of the loved hills of his childhood and the eternal valley will live in harmony, and greed will be forever banished.

Even in the depth of his sleep he vaguely senses he is neither the first nor the last to dream this way, and it gives him strength to know his father also dreamed it before his death, that the dream would irresistibly go on beyond his own life, that it was his powerful heritage, and that some day the dream would come to pass because it had outlived the plagues and wars and was present even on the dreadful night before the vultures feasted.

Now, as always, a new day began and he awakened from his long sleep. He lay a while on his warm cot next to the clay ground stepped on so often that it was smooth and hard. As he opened his eyes he looked up at the half-finished roof of his hovel. It still needed much more work to become a house, but during the next holiday, when he would not have to sell his labor to the factory, it would be his turn. Then all his friends, neighbors who like himself were building homes, would come to help him.

If, in the meantime, they could gather enough construction materials, the little house would be finished before the rains came and then he and his wife and the four small ones could live comfortably. Two of his friends would bring wood planks and tiles; another would bring nails; another sand; another cement. Each had offered to bring something, knowing in advance where to obtain the processed materials, by exchanging for something not needed or working after the main job, or begging or, more often than not, stealing wherever possible.

In a few months they would finish two more rooms, perhaps later cover the ground with tiles of different colors and shapes. After all that was finished they could indulge in the great luxury of building a little patio behind the house.

Half asleep, he smiled.

He heard the barefoot steps of his wife, the light rustling of her dress as she went about the room preparing breakfast, now pumping the bellows, starting the fire. He swallowed, thinking of the hot *aguapanela*, the brown sugar in water, that would give him the strength to work. Day was long and work hard, and he would not have more to eat until the evening. Maybe there was a piece of corn bread this morning. Feeling the rumbling of his stomach, he asked his woman about the bread and smiled when she answered yes, there would be corn bread today. Beseeched by the urgency to swallow again, he thought how he would savor his breakfast, seeing himself holding the *totuma* filled to the brim with the sweet liquid, clutching it close to himself to let the heat pass through his hands and chest into his body and imagining how he would place his face over the steam to fill his lungs with the penetrating aroma, closing his eyes in anticipation of the exquisite taste.

He did not want to think about the solid corn bread that would give him strength for the new day of work; the salty *arepa* with its hard crust making a crunchy sound when he bit, feeling the heaviness as it went down his throat, well chewed, past the point where hunger was pacified, where the food would be taken into his own body and become part of it; where no one could seize it from him.

He wanted to keep the corn bread for last as a surprise, as a secret gift to himself. He should not have asked his wife about it because the surprise would no longer be there. Yet it was good to know in order to make preparations. At last he decided to pretend there would be no corn bread this morning. Maybe it would feel like a surprise anyway.

"Today you can grumble, old stomach! Let the little juices flow—let them prepare the way!"

It was still very early in the morning and it was hard to see. But now that a small and quivering flame began to brighten the hearth, the room appeared softly lit and the shadows slowly began to move into their hiding places in the corners. His wife was wise not to use up the candles. They were for very special occasions. Maybe after his friends had helped him with the work they would all sit in the back of the hovel in what might some day become a patio. Then he would ask his wife for a candle to be placed in the center of the circle of seated friends, and cover it with a bright, red paper globe that would shine as though it were a holiday. He thought how the shadows would move around the lighted candle, how all his friends would feel tired and happy, telling jokes, drinking beer they would somehow obtain and singing ballads from the mountains. He knew his wife would save at least one of the candles to light the Virgin's image. He automatically made the sign of the cross over his body thinking about the Virgin. But he still wouldn't let his wife use the two candles for her: one must be saved for the party. He smiled, thinking how this image of the Virgin was the only possession among all the objects they had which was neither stolen nor begged for. Yes, it was true that they paid for the food they ate and for most of the cheap clothes they wore. And he would also have to pay for years to come the mortgage on the small lot he had finally rescued from the swamps where he was now building his home. What he earned at the factory was barely enough to pay for the rags and monthly mortgage. A few cents remained for food and his wife was clever enough to grow most of the vegetables in the small garden behind the hovel. Frequently he stole. All the materials to build the little house and the furniture had been stolen, which is why there was such a diversity of styles. Nothing really matched but it was better than the tin boxes and cardboards of the hillsides where he spent his childhood. His eyebrows knitted tensely as he thought of the hard work he did at the textile factory to pay the debt for the ground.

It was true that the factory owners had paid most of the initial costs to dry the neighboring land, pumping the water out of the swampy lowlands and building the drains into the river. But they had bought the immersed land for next to nothing and the project became a profitable investment for them. It also kept the workers close to the factory, and paying monthly installments.

It reminded him of the way the old, sweaty coins were handed out to him when he was a child: grudgingly, almost with loathing, wanting to get rid of something that bothered their consciences. The handouts were barely enough to keep him alive, extending him a momentary help that was only sufficient to assuage the beggar's fury, plugging his rebellious mouth with a few crumbs, postponing his protest, dulling his secret designs to attack, to strike out, to finish them off once and for all with their damn structure of endless legal bullshit with which they subdued him. He and his neighbors were paying dearly and he was afraid they would always keep him indebted. They were cunning enough to ease his terrible load a little here, a trifle there, bringing about what they called the great reforms every twenty years and for which he also paid, since they increased the cost of his daily life so that at the end of the accounting the so-called reforms turned out to be nothing more than lies and crumbs, just enough to keep his anger chained, to always make him work for them and pay them with the sweat of his life.

"They steal from me and I take only what's mine," he thought dissatisfied, feeling badly because he was so poor and could not build his house without stealing. He tried to think of something else, annoyed with himself for having thought of his poverty again and the work he did for the profit of others, realizing that he was a thief. He got up and took water out of an earthen pot, briskly splashing his face and pouring some over his back. Trying to forget his poverty he remembered the dream he had between his sleep and his awakening and told it to his wife.

"All the night," he said, touching her, "all the night, I dreamed of the good and peaceful life, without violence and work that kills, to give to the children the things that last, so the good life could be for them also, not only for the rich."

She paused in her work and looked at him for the first time on this new day. "All of us have the same dream," she answered.

And she went to awaken her four children who slept huddled on a mattress in a corner. She embraced each tenderly, playfully rubbing her face against them. When they arose, half-asleep, she turned her serious face toward her husband, adding:

"The rich ones, when they were poor, also dreamed the same."

He looked into the fire, waiting for his breakfast.

"Almost none of them had real needs, they were rich already when they were born."

He combed his fingers through his hair and kept talking:

"I wonder what is the thought of the rich man now."

"Maybe he dreams you will stop your dreaming and work harder for him." She laughed bitterly, feeling she had sinned, sensing the heaviness of hatred in her heart against the rich man. And then she felt forced to add:

"Maybe they dreamed so long ago they don't even remember." She felt a little better for saying these words, defending those she knew did not deserve to be defended.

They remained silent. While she stirred the sweetened water, the woman thought how she might be late for Mass and how she would have to confess the hatred that boiled in her for a few moments against the rich. The good priest would forgive her. The penitence would be small, maybe just one Hail Mary.

The man sat beside her looking into the fire, silently thinking how he would feel if he were the owner of a great fortune, a man of importance who would be called white and doctor even if his skin was dark and he had no diploma of any kind; or director of some bank, or member of an old, prominent family known and respected by everyone, going to luxurious places and eating in expensive restaurants whenever he had the urge, ordering a plate of blood pudding, an order of mountain beefsteak, one of those tasty ears of corn with rib of pig, and beans with buttered hoofs and a fried banana for dessert, with the usual little wine, red, hurry it up because I'm starved. For my wife she'd like, wouldn't you?, hind leg of lamb singed over hot coals with bacon but without beans, and also guava paste and small salty cheese for dessert and a soft drink, and for the two bigger boys let's see what do the boys want to eat?, bring the big one a chine of pork, the duck over flame to this one, and to the little one a suckling pig, very tender, and soft drinks since they all like that, and don't forget the meat pies and a few buttered corn breads.

Self-absorbed, he was looking at the pieces of corn bread being warmed over in the hearth. Forcing himself out of his reverie, he asked again:

"But what happened to the rich, why did they change if ever they were poor?"

"The silver," she answered. "The silver changed them, made them forget. They couldn't help it."

He got up and looked intensely into her eyes. "I wouldn't change," he said resolutely. "Do you think we would change? And forget what it is to be poor?"

"The silver kills. That's why God only gives it to a few."

But he wanted her to answer and repeated:

"I wouldn't change. I would never forget."

"All say the same but all change," she said. And seeing her man's face turn somber upon hearing what she said, added:

"There are only a few who will never forget." But in her heart she doubted. She hurried to serve the breakfast.

The man stretched out his eager hands to receive from his woman the large, steaming vessel which he placed upon his knees first and then brought up and held close to his chest. He bent over it, ceremoniously closing his eyes, inhaling the sweet smell and breathing the damp heat that went down into his lungs. He felt just as he had hoped he would feel.

He breathed deeply as he took the first mouthful, slurping noisily with his lips, chewing the sweet liquid, holding it in his mouth for a while and swallowing slowly, expanding his chest and feeling how the warmth descended into his stomach, thinking about how he would leave the corn bread he clutched greedily against his chest for last.

And he forgot everything he had said, thought, or felt that dawn.

VIII
THE MAIDEN

SHE ESCAPED FROM THE TORMENTING HUNGER OF the tin and cardboard houses of the hills and counted herself among the fortunate. At an early age, defenseless and inexperienced, she gained admission as a maid's helper into one of the mansions of the mighty, to earn there her food and lodging.

She clearly heard the shuffling of feet moving with awkward slyness in the silent corridors of the night, outside the door that was her protection. That door provided her only privacy and she had mistakenly believed it would always shield her, offering a little place of security and comfort to hide her blossoming girl's body from the daily curiosity with which she increasingly was regarded by men.

She heard her door open surreptitiously. She sensed the presence of the man inside her room, calling her by name even though he had never deigned to speak a word to her that was not an order or a demand during the many days she brought breakfast or served the family's dinner. She knew this feared boss of hers whom she had never dared to look in the eyes and who now was in this darkness, desired her with an unrelenting urgency.

She had often heard from older girls how all maids are sooner or later taken by their masters or their masters' sons. She had laughed at the gossip, those whisperings, observing the knowing looks, pretending to understand everything when in reality she was so innocent she grasped nothing of what they spoke, and she had enjoyed the fascination produced in her by what was forbidden, what was always enshrouded in a youthful mystery, seeming to indicate something dangerous but pleasurable. However, the real significance of all this talking, the tragedy it did not speak of, remained for her a peculiar secret she could not unravel. It began to make her restless, producing a misgiving bordering on fear if only because it was an unknown thing, alien to her ways. And she worried because there had always been something foreboding about this way of talking in murmurs, something that made the older, more experienced girls sad in spite of their laughter as they said: "They wasted me and I am now ruined in the happy life forever."

She could not understand why the older girls felt branded for life and condemned to wander through the endless streets of the city at night, abused and insulted by men. And why did they call such a life a happy one?

When she realized she must give to this man what he wanted, she was also afraid of the pain she had heard from her friends was part of the first time, when one lost her virginity, the pain which her imagination and superstition had built into an unfathomable monster, terrifying her and keeping her now silent, holding her breath, quivering under the blanket, peering through fingers tightly pressed against her eyes, hoping that the figure looming in the dark, swaying and whispering, would vanish and never bother her again.

She attempted to conjure up the image of the sweet, tranquil face of her favorite Virgin, the same benefactress to whom she had always prayed when needing help or consolation, the one with the tender gaze who understood everything, to whom she began to pray to free her from danger. But the menacing figure, instead of vanishing as she expected, came closer.

In the dark he squatted in his drunkenness, unable to focus his eyes, still feeling mischievous and playful, jovial as he had felt at the party in his favorite club and, upon hearing the childish murmur of her prayer, he began to laugh with a hoarse sound he attempted to muffle while he whispered:

"Don't be afraid, beautiful dove, your *papacito* will not hurt you."

He laughed again, unable to stop. He saw the image of himself and of his opulent friends when they all were young, riding on horseback over sierras of his family's hacienda, lassoing whatever unwary peasant girls happened to cross their path to take them for their collective, sporting pleasure. Finally, focused on his glassy stare and with the urge to proceed now with greater zeal, he approached her in anticipation of this newest episode in his comfortable life, another adventure, always excusable because he was drunk and because she was in his service and would anyway, sooner or later, be used and wasted by men.

She continued praying as she heard his whispered, coaxing words and his muffled laughter in that alarming stillness, knowing that the two of them were alone that night in this enormous house. Fear came over her now more forcefully as she felt his panting breath. She had never been alone in the depth and solitude of night with a man in a small room, and not in her remotest fantasy did she ever imagine that her first one would be as old and drunk as this, nor one who, if she refused, could exile her back to the living poverty of the hills, to the mendacity of the street, and put an end to the food she stole every day from his abundant pantry so her family would not die of hunger.

Now that he was so close to her that she could smell the bitterness of alcohol and tobacco and the sweaty odor of the old man's body, she turned her head toward the wall burying her face in a pillow, feeling that perhaps she could commit her soul to the everlasting protection of her little Virgin and let him at the same time use her flesh any way he wished, without looking at him, without witnessing what was happening. As she allowed him to possess her, she discovered—with the shattered desire of youth that aged suddenly before having lived—that for her there would be no beautiful prince offering a gallant arm through the veiled forest, that bells would not toll in her honor, nor would she ever hear the loving words, and that neither the strange promise of the eternal, pure flowers, nor the sweet taste of the fruit would be granted to her.

She understood in the darkness that this secret and wet urgency, panting and vulgar, of a man with a large family, feared for his great fortune and importance among the powerful of his land, this sweaty tug and impotent jostling by this old and drunken man with granddaughters older than herself and whose demands she dared not disobey, was part of an existence more sordid and turbulent than she had ever known in the hills, in the corners of the streets where she had begged from the time of her birth, or had thought possible in her innocence.

She let him do to her everything his indurate gluttony desired. And feeling his trembling hands touch her nakedness, his greedy lips and tongue incessantly burn her flesh in all its youthful vulnerability, she felt at last dragged as in an uncontainable current which also invaded her, shaking her body for a few seconds of rapid and untamed surge of pleasure, almost as part of an unreal extension of herself, as a compromise between the aspirations of her lost youth and the unbending reality that was now for the first time entering and becoming an inextricable part of her life. Even as her lips, hidden in the pillow, uttered quietly the last words of her prayer, it became clear to her that this man and she were now united in some unspoken and undefined way in mortal sin, like two conspirators, against her Virgin.

And as she experienced the convulsive straining within herself and the flow of her virtue's blood, her previous fears were replaced by a new, infinitely more overwhelming dread, which seized her completely as she thought how this old man and herself might now suddenly die in this sweaty embrace as punishment and find themselves burning in the bowels of Hell together, as she had been taught, before the very eyes of God and of her Virgin, like faded blades of grass.

"Bendita tu eres entre todas las mujeres y bendito sea el fruto de tu vientre..."—Blessed art Thou among women and blessed be the fruit of Thy womb...

Virgen de Guadalupe: Daunted by the taste of dry bones tormenting our tongues and the wailing of dying leaves roaring in our ears, let us drink from the fresh mirror of the arroyo once again and listen to the sound of blood.

Protect us, oh Virgen del Carmen, from the jackal and the alligator who tear our living flesh, smiling, lest our corpses be crowned with teeth, lest we give birth to slaves.

Virgen de la Asunción: When will the wild and free horse neigh on the paramo and the eagle spread her wings on the summit? And when will we rest in the land of our ancestors with the dark and loved faces of our youth?

Virgen de los Desamparados: We are abandoned in the vortex of the sewers of a thousand cities and we have lost—oh, help us find—the odor of tangerines, the strawberry taste, and the little doll that cries and closes her eyes.

Walk with us, Virgen de la Soledad, among the nocturnal multitude, or at the end of the pale green street of the interminable dawn where our children play as beggars with the world's hunger sleeping in their throats.

Virgen de la Macarena: Was the blood of our brothers spilled upon the sands so we may host the swords that broke their horizons, that we may stare dumbly over the scab of the eternal beds?

Cleanse our impurity with your tears, Virgen de la Dolorosa, the soul of our sinful wombs. We were tempted by the seed of the conqueror and deserve the stone thrown from the shoulder and the look of the alms giver.

We have already eaten the flesh of our arms and have swallowed the kiss of tongue and the snake to give the bastard children our daily bread, Virgen de la Encarnación, but we beg you to spare them from turning into skeletons before the rich harvest.

Virgen de la Candelaria: will the light reach into the marshes and will the divine whisper of the humming bird stir the hidden flower within our breast before we become phantoms in the promised city of the new day?

Help us, help us, Virgen del Socorro, for the menacing pimps are closer and ready to prey on the open wound of the maidens with the dagger and the arrow, with the bistoury and the spear.

Place a drop of pity on our withered breasts, Virgen del Tequendama, on our flesh of torch in flames.

And if it be your will, oh, Virgen del Perpetuo, give us a crumb, any little piece of the everlasting bread in this solitude and a safe roof in the skies of our homeland.

God save Thee María, full of grace....Blessed be the fruit of Thy womb...

Amen.

In the impenetrable jungle not a single extra leaf fell from a tree, nor a single leaf less.

And on the other side of the universe, the magnificent star traced its gigantic orbit and rolled on—serene and ineluctable—just as it happened a million centuries ago.*

---

*Poem entitled "Unanswered prayer by the choir of young harlots" was published in A. Berger-Kiss's bilingual anthology *Voices from the Earth = Voces de la Tierra*, ECOE Ediciones, Bogotá, 1995.

FOURTH PART

IX
THE BARRIO

THEY ROAMED THE CITY NIGHT AND DAY AS though an eternal carnival had been decreed. The brashest swayed aggressively, trying to seduce men in any nook of the streets, scandalizing the mothers of adolescent boys who looked at them with furtive, covetous eyes. No matter how many times they were admonished by the police they continued wiggling their breasts and buttocks enticing patrons of shops, restaurants and theaters. They were even seen in churches tempting the faithful in the last few benches.

There wasn't a place in the city where the women didn't loiter, exhibiting their charms.

Their activities ignited sporadic and indignant editorials in the daily newspapers, often written at the instigation of religious and secular institutions whose self-proclaimed mission was to transform, without spending a penny, the wicked into worthwhile, obedient and reverent citizens.

Most recently, as attested by numerous handbills delivered by members of the police department from house to house, this noble cause had been adopted vociferously throughout the electoral campaign by the newly elected governor who had waged a battle without truce to fulfill his ambition.

The new governor based his campaign on a promise "to rid the city of this infernal pest of prostitutes who threaten the moral fiber of our society, as soon as I have the authority to act in response to the conscience of the people."

No one knew, nor did they bother to find out, how the new governor obtained authorization to recruit policemen on duty as propagandists of his campaign while they were in the payroll of his opponent's government, who after much intrigue, was defeated.

The new governor's campaign was not to be questioned. To debate it was to defy patriotic and ecclesiastic ideals. He threatened the use of force against prostitution, but there was no mentioning provision of jobs, rehabilitation, training, improvements in housing or of looking after the health needs of the citizenry. Since the nobility of his purpose was widely proclaimed from the pulpits of the city and the countryside and often in the secrecy of the confessionals, he was elected. Or, at least the votes were counted in such a way—in true native style as some of the more ironic observers said—that in the end he became the governor of the most industrial province in the republic.

No one presumed to know how the official vote counters were endowed with a devilish magnetism which included the power to transform the visible into invisible, how they possessed the shrewdness of wizards without rival and were experts in the cabalistic arts of black magic, or what supernatural spells bestowed upon them the uncanny ability to change votes from one candidate to another before the presence of so many witnesses whose eyes, hardly blinking, were glued on the ballot boxes to prevent tampering. They watched the official counters unwrap, one by one, the ribbons that tied the boxes, breaking the seals stamped on the fissures with a variety of multicolored and official stamps which could not be ripped except in the august presence of the seven cuckolds from the community representing the great free people. The official counters signed receipts with an air of majesty each step of the way, noting in ink on a separate sheet of paper the count of each vote, one at a time, without the aid of counting machines, three times repeatedly and separately by three different prestidigitators so as to wind up with a number which would be scientifically reliable, exact, according to updated statistical procedures, to prevent anyone from pulling a wicked fraud on The People, since after all this is a great Democracy, a sovereign virtuous state, an example without parallel in all the hemisphere, and we're not gonna let anyone soil our institutions and take away from us goddammit the privilege of free men!

Daily the new governor practiced the art of looking dignified, often with the aid of a full-length mirror his wife imported for their living room. He was known as a descendant of one of the first immigrants from Spain to settle in the valley, an old man who constantly traveled out of the country because he felt cosmopolitan and disdained the provincialism of the tropics. There was another reason for undertaking so many trips to New York and Zurich. He deposited large amounts of money in secret accounts, the exorbitant profits of his family's factories. "Life around here," he confided to his closest friends, who behaved likewise, "in this homeland of ours, is no longer safe and the day we least expect it some stupid revolution might blow up right in our faces and a herd of ungrateful workers and angry poor—the unwashed mob—might rob us the fruits of our efforts." It is true that the governor was able to entice foreign investors into trusting him with their capital for mutual benefit, creating many alliances in the name of progress which, after all the rhetoric turned out to be nothing more than bare-faced conspiracies against his less fortunate compatriots whose cheap labor he contracted with the foreigners' money. His latest project with overseas investors was the building of an enormous modern hotel in the center of the city with all the conveniences of the glittering world, a hotel that would charge for one day's stay in its luxurious rooms the equivalent of a year's salary of a construction laborer. Now, that was profit! Just thinking about it in front of the mirror put a smile on his face from ear to ear.

No sooner was the governor elected then, according to long established tradition, he sought audience with the archbishop to pay his respects, receive a public blessing, and leave a private contribution of substantial proportions which he and his illustrious family had pledged during the course of the electoral campaign to show his undying gratitude and loyalty to the high principles of love, human dignity, and justice and freedom for our people. Such was his public eulogy, quoted in the newspapers.

The governor introduced the members of his staff to all the dignitaries present, which consisted of his most intimate cronies from industry and commerce, all flashing their best smiles before the cameras. All who were present, including the high ranking military and police officials with collections of shiny decorations of medals and ribbons impressively adorning their impeccable uniforms, and members of the curia in reverent file according to their rank and seated behind the archbishop, greeted each other with courtesies and brief nods and toasts made with grandiloquent gestures of supreme elegance. It was then that the archbishop, who only a few hours before had demonstrated his humility by publicly washing the feet of twelve prisoners hauled in for the ceremony from one of the local jail houses, representing the twelve apostles, rose and decided to bless all those present before the various television cameras and newspapers, sprinkling everyone in sight with holy water as he placed himself in what he conceived was a position of sanctity and asked Our Lord to guide the thoughts and actions of this new servant of the Republic and of our great society according to the noble and spiritual heritage of his ancestors who, as is well known, have always lived up to the highest principles and maintained the immaculate ethical standards of our democratic sovereign Republic, for the honor and everlasting pride of our exalted lineage.

This exchange of verbiage stirred those present, especially the new governor, who imagined himself to be the central figure of a memorable event of national proportions which would appear on the front pages of many newspapers and magazines with wide-reaching circulation. But since everyone present was so self-engrossed in his own importance and the role he must play, each felt it necessary to maintain an air of constant vigilance, expecting to be photographed at any instant or suddenly thrust into an interview with the anchor of a popular television news program, carefully turning the head to exhibit the photogenic side and all of them smiling like great men of the world with the comprehensive and beatific smile of alligators who have just finished breakfast, hardly deigning to look at one another, maintaining an air of detached refinement, sobriety and what was considered to be the physical and psychological embodiment of what they so often referred to as human dignity.

And were it not for the fact that even before the day-long ceremonies were over a special assistant to the governor was dispatched with great urgency to hand his puppet at the State Assembly a small piece of wrinkled paper with a message saying, "Church and military backing us fully. Introduce the new ordinance regarding the prostitutes immediately," a candid spectator or reader of the next day's newspapers would have erroneously concluded that the whole affair had been carried out to emphasize a charming tradition, an innocent and truly unforgettable event reflecting the piety and grace of those called upon to govern or who were leaders of the society.

The following day the newspapers of the city and many parts of the republic proclaimed the extraordinary news:

"Yesterday the State Assembly approved a

resolution regulating several aspects of morality and public welfare. Signed by the newly elected governor, appearing with representatives of finances and officers of the Army and the Police Department to receive the Archbishop's blessing, (see photo) the resolution is referred to as one for public women because it's designed to control the grave problem of prostitution in our state.

"It has been widely known and it has been openly discussed during the past elections that there are grave social problems caused by so many women on our public streets who have persisted, in spite of innumerable warnings, in perverting the citizenry with acts of public immorality, scandalizing with profane conduct and corrupting our youth, glory and promise of our homeland. Since these women—many of them minors—have been repeatedly admonished without results by our distinguished and responsible civil as well as ecclesiastic authorities whose social conscience is well respected, and since the morality and Christian spirit of our lineage are in imminent danger of being soiled, the State Assembly approved a decree regarding the public women, thereby creating the following resolution which will become effective today and which will be enforced by the Municipal Police and the Armed Forces:

"Resolution Concerning Public Women
and Zones of Tolerance.

"Article One. The only designated zone of tolerance for street walkers will be the region of the city commonly known as 'the lowlands' which has been rescued from the marshes and river and which encompasses an isolated area of approximately forty square blocks in the southern outskirts of the city.

"Article Two. All red light districts or zones of tolerance will no longer be so designated, beginning with the date of this resolution.

"Article Three. Without exception, all public women who are living or soliciting outside the new zone of tolerance must proceed to obtain residence in the zone designated in Article One beginning today.

"Article Four. Public women living in zones of tolerance that were defined as such prior to this date will have fifteen (15) days, beginning today, to move into the zone designated in Article One.

"Article Five. Saloons presently in existence within the tolerance zone designated in Article One and saloons that will open there in the future can remain open at all hours without time restrictions. Outside the newly created tolerance zone saloons must close at 12 o'clock midnight.

"Article Six. Violations of any Article of this resolution will be punished with ten (10) days of unappealable detention for the first violation and twenty (20) days of unappealable detention for any subsequent violation.

"Article Seven. Any prior resolution regarding the issues described in these Articles contrary to the present one is hereby invalidated.

"Approved by the President of the State Assembly, the Municipal Mayor, and the Secretary of State, this resolution shall be executed with the support of state authorities as of this date."

It was not mentioned by the resolution or in newspaper accounts that the neighborhood known as "the lowlands" had grown over many years into the residential sector for workers of the textile factory which competed with the enterprises of the newly elected governor's family.

So swift and unchecked was the drop in stock prices of the factory now suddenly within the tolerance zone, that it was generally assumed it would be dissolved and the pieces merged into the growing monopoly of its competitor.

The small print in the body of the resolution also called for residents of the lowlands to provide a place for the activities of the public women to prevent them from spreading their immorality and disorder in the rest of the city. Residents who refused would be compelled to sell their property to the highest bidder. The message, without the legal double-talk, simply meant, "Turn your homes into whorehouses or get out."

Laborers from the textile factory located in the lowlands and residents of the area hastily formed a committee to ask the government for the reasons it chose their neighborhood as the tolerance zone for prostitution. The curt answer they received from one of the governor's subordinates was that according to a recent sociological study, the great majority of their neighborhood's residents lived in common law. Although they professed to be married and most of them had several children, their unions had never been legalized by either the State or the Church. Consequently, their ties were not recognized; they were committing adultery and living in sin. It meant, according to the government spokesman, that the life style of the residents was in the eyes of decent, Christian citizens, just another form of prostitution. That being the case according to the paralogic of the argument, other prostitutes who engaged in such activities more openly, might as well join them.

"In reality," the government agent concluded, "what the State has done in passing this resolution is to put a seal of tolerance on what has been occurring in the lowlands for many years." Having said that, he proceeded to inundate his listeners with a flood of irrelevant statistics.

The factory in the lowlands experienced a devaluation of its real estate holdings in the neighborhood and its functioning was impaired by the exodus of workers' families which made finding trained labor difficult. A complete deterioration of neighborhood activities ensued. Chaos followed, forcing the total isolation of the entire lowlands by the armed forces to protect the citizens since the new zone of tolerance fell into the hands of hoodlums.

The city's police not only picked up all women who walked the streets soliciting, but after the fifteen days of grace mentioned in the 4th Article of the new resolution, invaded houses of prostitution in other parts of the city, taking the women by force in wagons or marching them handcuffed to each other in long lines across the city and letting them loose in the barrio of tolerance which overflowed at an alarming rate.

Many of the captured women were minors who had been trapped in the streets while innocently going about their own business. Many a family whose adolescent girl disappeared went frantically searching for their lost child among the prostitutes that flowed like a river into the desecrated neighborhood.

No one counted carefully because no census was possible under the chaotic circumstances of the invasion, but many observers who witnessed the events after the new regulations regarding public women took effect said that the initial influx of women to the lowlands on that first week was over ten thousand. At the end of the month there were countless more.

The women arrived in a frantic rush by the truckload, in cars, and mostly on foot, dragging trunks and cots through the streets, helped sometimes by their pimps. The gaping citizenry watched in perplexed stupefaction as events never before known in their city unfolded. The disorganization in the neighborhood was total. As more women and girls came to live within the confines of the new tolerance zone, curiosity seekers were attracted, especially the spirited young men of the city and its vicinity, creating an outrageous spectacle.

The entire neighborhood was fenced with ropes and surrounded by the police. Once inside the encircled area none of the women were allowed to leave. Distressed parents of girls who had disappeared had to get special permits to free their children. Often these permits took days to obtain.

What had been a barrio of humble and hard working people was turned into a frenzied pandemonium. Swarms of roving street sellers pushing their carts, announcing their goods and foodstuff, some cooking in the middle of the streets on makeshift stoves, lent a feverish air of forced carnival to the barrio.

An opposition movement was hastily formed by residents with the immediate objective of not allowing their homes to be confiscated, waiting for the protection of the courts of justice, hoping that people would finally come to their senses and stop the madness unleashed against them. But the only solitary voice that came in their defense, though forcefully spoken in the floor of the senate at the capital of the republic, was not heard, must less heeded.

The workers' movement created, for a few weeks, a spirit of resistance. For many days most of the women who had been thrust upon the neighborhood were unable to find lodging in the houses of the workers, although many, using their charms, seduced more than one family head into sharing a bed.

Thousands of tents went up overnight throughout the streets of the barrio. Planks of wood reinforced with metal plates, aluminum sheets, and discarded pieces of corroded metal and cardboard glistened in the light of the new day. The neighborhood seemed to be a city of miniature dwellings which, like a voracious cancer, infiltrated every vacant spot, filling completely the empty lots and the sidewalks as well as the main streets, leaving no room for traffic. The only space left was the narrow corridors among the squalid and degrading crowded structures. The biggest slum the city had ever known was created within a week, with criminal behavior running rampant night and day, women brazenly enticing into any available corner the half drunk customers who crawled everywhere in search of cheap thrills to calm their lust.

The doors of the neighborhood homes remained bolted for a long time, the dwellers maintaining what they called "the siege of decency," covering their windows and doors with placards and handmade announcements glued against the walls, written crudely with awkward and untrained letters. The residents, lacking a formal education as most of them were, wrote phrases filled with grammatical and spelling errors, all very visible products of the distress in their vain attempt to communicate with a deaf and blind world. It was upon these bits of paper and cardboard that people, who had never written before, expressed openly their worries, protests, threats, supplications and thoughts, and felt for the first time the oppressive anxiety of seeing their efforts torn to shreds, spat upon and spread out like trash on the streets by the multitude of women, pimps, customers and government agents who were intent on turning the peaceful working class barrio into a red-light district.

A young reporter of one of the city's newspapers was able to copy some of the announcements in his notebook before they were destroyed but the publishers refused to print the report or reproduce his notes, saying that the sentiments expressed by the residents of the invaded barrio did not deserve to be published because they were poorly written. The young writer swore that whatever happened to him he would someday find a way to publish the anguished bits of broken literature written by the humble of his homeland:

This is MY Home and RESPECT! pleas.
We die befor letin then beat us
GOD Dear BLESED will love us if not you
this is NOT a house of whores.
DO NOT PERVRT THE CHILDRN.

THERE NO WOMIN HERE—KEEP OUT

We are poor but good.
Our HUMAN RIGHTS must be protected.
I will kill—the—first—one—who—comes—in!
Our HoMe—Dear HoMe OUR YES! OUR?
The Government protects only the rich.

The Virgin Is Our Holy Mother
we bilt this hom by bit and will not give it up esept in bits

THIS HOUSE IS A PRIVATE RESIDENCE—NOT PUBLIC

Long live **FREEDOM!**
Those who live by the sord die by the sord.

This house NOT for sale—to nobody!
would you do this to your MOTHER?
Lawas are made by the rich **against** the Poor.

What was built in 20 yr can't be distroid in 1 day.
In the name of GOD merciful we beg you not to harm our children—they are innocent of all sens—you love your children and we love OUR.

With BLOOD we bilt +++++ with BLOOD we win

Dont distroey thi lif of our chaild
LONG LIVE THE RIGHTS OF MEN!
Siners—go to HELL!

SICK PERSON INSIDE DO NOT MOLEST

Down with the BRUTAL law!
Fr yer's we werkt an it our OWN HOME
Damn those who persecute the poor.
We ar wrkrs— let's wrk in pes.
The RICH will someday pay for this
we are poor but also desent

LONG LIVE OUR HOMELAND !!!!!!!

(Note: "The Resolution Concerning Public Women and Zones of Tolerance" was enacted and carried out by the authorities in Medellín, Colombia in 1953.)

X
THE PRIEST

ALTHOUGH HE WAS THE PARISH PRIEST OF THE lowlands, neither the ecclesiastic nor the civil authorities informed him of the transformations that would take place in the barrio. When his neighbors came to tell him that the lowlands would become a red-light district, he could not believe the news. But a few hours after the decree regarding the streetwalkers appeared and when the women began to arrive in the district by the hundreds, when he saw them loitering in the streets, lying aggressively on the grass in the empty lots between the houses, when the music from the taverns, with its pulsating and deafening beat invaded the peacefulness of the chapel and the adjacent room he occupied, he felt frustrated not knowing how to defend his poverty-stricken parishioners.

He prayed devoutly before doing anything else, as was his custom, making promises to God he was sure he could keep in exchange for divine assistance. He surmised that he would need much help in this matter because it was something he couldn't understand and was completely outside the problems he was used to solving.

He decided to sacrifice for a whole year his weekly visits to his secular home, his family's mansion on the other side of the city. This was the home where he had spent his life in the lap of luxury until the day he entered the seminary and where he loved to go for a rest when his ecclesiastic duties became overwhelming. He went there to protect himself from the hardships of his vocation.

He prayed for a whole hour, a little annoyed that the music didn't stop and peace was not restored. He was a gentle man whose words brought a great calm to the needy families of the neighborhood and whose generosity toward the poor was thoroughly acknowledged in the parish.

He shook his head, pained because the problem had not vanished. So often, difficulties worked out just as he had asked, almost miraculously. But God knew his heart better than he knew himself, he thought, closing his eyes again.

Perhaps this tribulation would unexpectedly become a test of faith. If he at least could pray well, if his words had the eloquence of the great saints of the Church, if his phrases were as erudite as those of a sage, or as sublime as those of a poet, perhaps they would penetrate that termite-eaten roof, would scurry among the leaves of the trees and, rising above the clouds, arrive straight at the very throne of God on the other side of the universe to be heard above all this infernal music which didn't even allow him to think.

Maybe he shouldn't make offers to his God: Will you give me this if I sacrifice that? His confessor had chided him gently for trying to make deals with God during his seminary days. It was a bad habit, a foolish reaction when he felt helpless. He was a man now, he told himself. But what harm was there in making promises, especially ones he could keep? He certainly didn't want to trick God. For a long time he had fulfilled every promise he had made to God in his supplications. He wouldn't let himself forget the time he had disappointed God with an unkept promise.

The incident happened during the year after he entered the seminary as a very young man just out of high school many years ago, before his final examinations. Since he hadn't been able to keep his promises then, he got sick with intermittent fevers which no physician could diagnose and sporadic attacks of diarrhea which left him completely exhausted and unable to sleep for weeks. He considered himself divinely punished. Keeping promises became one of his most sacred private laws; his personal pact with God, he thought proudly. And now, when he heard the reckless yells from the street surging repeatedly with renewed vigor like the waves of an irrepressible tide, he wondered whether he should offer another sacrifice, enlarge his part of the bargain.

He plugged his ears with cotton and closed his eyes, wishing with all his powers of concentration that the unleashed evil against his parish would disappear. But when he listened again, the fictitious and transient peace created by plugging his ears was shattered, pierced continually by the strident music that vibrated, fathomless and terrifying, with a confused and wanton pattern in which the savage and lascivious pulsations of several different rhythms were aimlessly mixed. Yes, he must pray more, sacrifice something that would truly hurt him, something that would be anchored in the very depths of his being and which would mark his life irreparably.

He felt the edge of a nail sticking into his skin as he knelt before the huge crucifix and he hoped that God would surely see and take pity on his pain, that He would appreciate his sacrificial tribute and help him solve the problem. For a moment he forgot about the commotion outside as he drove his knee against the nail until he felt the flow of blood.

When his parishioners came into the chapel he was still kneeling, moving his lips in an exaggerated way, crossing himself now and then. They waited impatiently at a distance, shifting their weight from one foot to the other restlessly, coughing to get his attention because they didn't dare call to him. He knew they were waiting for him, that they would ask for his help, and he felt distressed at not knowing what to do. But his intentions were good and everyone knew he was a charitable man. He thought God would help him at the decisive moment, that He would give him strength of spirit and understanding, that in the last instant he would receive divine inspiration.

He would have liked to remain kneeling all day and night, feeling the cruelty of the piercing nail mortifying his knee instead of facing the overwhelming demands of his congregation. He thought of the saints who sacrificed their lives for noble causes and for a moment wished to die crucified with his Christ, and told himself that if the opportunity were offered he would gladly give his life to lessen in the slightest the pain suffered by his Savior.

At last they began to call his name, at first under their breath and when they received no answer, summoned their courage until a murmur of voices clamored for his attention:

"Father! Father! Come help us!"

It was then he felt obligated to suspend his bargaining with God as a way to escape the present reality. He got up and came close to them, pretending to be surer of himself than he was, but not aiming to deceive them, just looking at them paternally to instill courage and hope. As he approached, they surrounded him submissively, kneeling as they had always done to ask his blessing.

After they received the blessing one of the men stood up. "What shall we do, Father?" the man asked. "The authorities decided to turn our homes into houses of prostitution. They are trying to force us to sell our homes, *Padrecito*. It's all we have. We built the houses with our own hands and with what they pay for them now we couldn't buy another house anywhere else in the city. Help us stop them, Father. What can we do if they kick us out? And where will we go? Who will protect us?" The others listened in silence, nodding their heads from time to time, the women crying, moving their lips in continuous prayer, passing trembling fingers over their rosaries.

"Faith, hope and charity," the priest told them, "are the qualities of the good Christian. But above all, my children, we must have faith: faith in God and in the Holy Church. We will always receive divine protection if our faith remains." And before they had the chance to make another demand, he led them to the altar kneeling again, searching with his knee for the consoling and cruel head of the nail and praying out loud this time, trying to drown out the sound of the pagan and sensual music from the street.

His parishioners knelt around him, hoping for his special powers to come forth, expecting some supernatural force to save them from the injustice hanging over their humble neighborhood, reverently believing that if anyone could help them, this priest would somehow do it. For they remembered the many times he had come to console them in the depth of the interminable night of sickness or when death had visited them. Kneeling there, with the light from the altar plainly on his face, he looked like one of the saints pictured on the sheets distributed during the catechism hour. By the altar's light, with his high-pitched voice that couldn't hide the fear stalking him, the priest appeared even younger than he was. Seeing him this way they realized his fragility, how afraid he was. But in some way he would also help them now, since he had always understood their suffering and had advised them with care and compassion. And the priest looked at them realizing his impotence before such calamitous events in this incomprehensible situation which was as new for him as it was for everyone else, something his teachers in the seminary had never taught him to resolve.

He felt saddened because he knew he must give them some kind of counsel, something concrete instead of just words, and he didn't have the faintest idea how to lessen their difficulties nor did he know the path to guide them. He continued praying, watching his flock surreptitiously, observing how the majority of the women, dressed in black, kissed the floor as they knelt, and the men standing, holding their hats in their hands with their ponchos carefully folded over their shoulders, forming a line, looked ready to wage a battle, although a few of them knelt with bowed heads and reverent expressions or with a supplicant look fixed on the purple wounds of the crucified Christ. And he remembered tenderly the ideals of youth, the constant yearning of his childhood and adolescence to become a priest in the midst of a flock of penitents, surrounded by their love, confident that he would help them find the road to salvation.

A busload of women got off in front of the chapel and their savage and profane screams assaulted the priest's ears, suddenly bringing him out of his self-absorption and reminding him of the necessity to take action. After he finished praying, the man who had spoken before said:

"Father, some of us organized a neighborhood committee this morning to ask the government its reasons for choosing our barrio as a haven for prostitutes and they told us that since most of those living here have not been legally married and live without the Church's blessing, they are—that is, we are—as sinful as any of the women of the happy life who sell their flesh in the streets. What do you say, Father?"

He had forgotten that detail, and hardly heard the question. Yes, it was true that the majority lived in sin because their union had never been sanctified by the sacrament of matrimony. It had never occurred to him because he had baptized so many children and buried so many of the old people who died in his parish. But it was the truth; they lived in sin without the indispensable blessing of the Church.

After so many years of living together they felt ashamed to ask the priest to marry them in the Church, after so much shared life. It was better not to speak of it. But now, the priest realized the majority of his parish had lived in sin for all those years before his very eyes. He never thought of them as being sinful. He grieved, feeling a heaviness burden his heart, and he asked himself if he had fallen short in his obligations. Perhaps he was responsible.

"Oh, my children," he said, "the ways of God are mysterious. We never know what his plans are for us, his poor servants, his flock. We are all sinners. I will always be ready to bless those who wish to consecrate their marriage at any time, day or night. Perhaps once your union is sanctified they will leave you alone."

Three hundred and fifty-five couples from the lowlands neighborhood—many with grown-up children and grandchildren present—gathered at the chapel to be married and blessed by the priest that same evening, but the wheels of injustice had made their inexorable move and there was no way to stop the authorities.

It was easy for them to see he was honest and that his heart was with them. But the man who had spoken before raised his voice again for the third time, saying, "Our Father, we ask you to join our committee and go with us to the governor's palace. We don't think it's fair that our homes be sold under duress for the pleasure of harlots and the business of pimps. Surely God is with us. We are working families. If you and the Church would join us they would stop tormenting us. We ask the Church to help us change this new law, put the women somewhere else if they have to have their red-light district. Not where our children are growing up. Come with us in our march, Father. Help us."

"I will help you the best I can," he answered. "But before joining your march I must ask the bishop's permission. In the meantime I will remain here for you. God will help us."

Realizing he was disappointing them, he added, shaking his head, "It isn't easy for the priest of a poor neighborhood. My heart and my blessing are with you, my beloved people, but I must remain here until I hear from my superiors. They know best."

Suddenly, he seized upon an idea and added, "Would some of you help me carry a loudspeaker? We could make a bigger noise to drown out their confounded music and devilish screaming." Some of the more fervent parishioners smiled shyly, like children whose pranks have not yet dealt their full blow of mischief, whose powers are yet untested and, particularly the women and those who were more pious, offered their help in carrying out the priest's plans.

Those who left tried to understand the reasons given by the priest for not participating in their committee's actions, excusing him and saying that after all, he could do no more for them without the support of his superiors. But the priest noticed when the man who had spoken for the others knelt to receive the blessing, his face was taut and black eyes dared to search his own, plumbing the depths of the priest's being like no one had done before. And when the worker got up from his bent knee to leave, the priest saw that the man did not cross himself as was the custom and as the others did. But the priest had accepted long ago the vow of obedience to his superiors and knew he could not do what his heart dictated in such public matters, but had to wait for orders from his superiors before proceeding. He loved his people and didn't try to hide from the man's scrutiny.

The worker went out into the street knowing he had rebelled against his Church when he refused to cross himself, when he had dared to search for the truth in the priest's heart with an affront he hadn't suspected he could muster. He was still surprised that those eyes hadn't tried to deceive him, escape his look or cover up what was inside, and that they had allowed him to look into the priest's most intimate being with a confidence and a love that now shamed him. That one is a good little priest, a good Father, the man thought, and I thought unfairly he was not to be trusted.

All day the priest and his helpers walked through the lowlands neighborhood as in a procession, carrying saints' busts on their shoulders while shouting prayers and admonitions into the loudspeaker in Spanish and a Latin that nobody understood, at best making only enough racket to drown out the music closest to them. But his momentary triumph brought him nothing but the ire of the women and their pimps, who began to ridicule him, shouting in their turn, the taverns turning up the music when he and his followers came near.

At the end of the day, he was hoarse and exhausted, frustrated by his lack of strength. He could barely speak. When he returned to his room, adjacent to the chapel, he had to listen all night to the furious shouting of those who came to wreak vengeance upon him for trying to oust them from the neighborhood. From time to time a rock would hit his door, startling him. The women took turns to ensure he wouldn't get any sleep, whispering vulgarities through the keyhole, trying to tempt him, offering themselves for his pleasure, saying to him repeatedly, "Under your cassock you must be a real man."

The priest heard them through the strongly bolted door in spite of having filled his ears with cotton and wrapped his head with a wool scarf given to him by an aunt for his last birthday when he became thirty-five years old.

The noise, the vengeful fury of those on the other side of the door, and his own anxiety wouldn't allow him to rest. Tears filled his eyes as he knelt with a prayer book and a crucifix in his hands, alone.

All night he cried and prayed while listening to the voices tempting him. Deep into the night, nearly overcome by the excitement and exhaustion of the last twenty-four hours he dozed while he prayed more calmly for the salvation of those who were plaguing him. But he woke again with the first light of dawn when he heard the surreptitious murmuring of women's coaxing voices, feigning lust calling for him beside his door. Then he noticed more clearly as he awakened out of his light slumber the unceasing agitation of the boisterous, savage music and all of the treachery loosed around him. He felt his knee and was aware of the intense pain there. He didn't dare move, even though his body began to shake. And picking up the crucifix that had slipped off the couch with one hand and holding the prayer book with the other, he stopped his ears with his knuckles, shouting the new prayer to cast aside temptation, feeling a living fear of the spiritual danger that confronted him in his own flesh. When dawn finally arrived to rescue him he begged some of his parishioners to take turns accompanying him, insisting that at least two of them stay with him wherever he went so that the women wouldn't torment him. They helped obediently, posting themselves much like guards by the closed door and chased the women away while he tried to sleep for a few hours unmolested by the drunken voices.

On the third day of the invasion, the community's school was closed by government decrees and the building converted into a clinic for the prevention of venereal diseases and a police station. Classrooms were turned into cells for prisoners on their way to the city's main prison.

Standing in front of what had been the school, the priest admonished the people to remember Christ's second coming and blessed the children as they evacuated the building. Just as the school's director handed the keys over to the police commander in the presence of the whole community, a long-awaited messenger arrived with the bishop's orders which the priest proceeded to read aloud and which, after a long preamble, said that he should lend no aid to the neighborhood committee "because it is a group which unfortunately has been deceived and led astray by outside communist agitators whose intention is to destroy our democratic and Christian way of life."

The bishop counseled him further by saying that the archbishop would be very pleased if he could organize a new committee of the faithful, a committee that truly represents the interests of the people in order to study the problems occurring in the neighborhood as reactions to the laws recently adopted by the Provincial Assembly.

He looked at the letter thoughtfully, wondering how he could carry out the task, and for a few seconds doubted the wisdom of the counsel he had just received, realizing that the strength of the neighborhood would be divided into two different factions, complicating the situation more than it was. He wondered where those outside political agitators referred to in the note had come from.

The priest began to recruit his most devoted assistants, reading them the bishop's message over and over and telling them it was like a voice from heaven calling on the chosen ones to unite in a just cause to change the entire course of their lives and inevitably bring them to God's very throne. And as the membership in the first committee shrunk as a result of his effort, the man who had refused to cross himself, the one with the deep and penetrating stare plumbing a soul's depth, came to speak with him again. This time the worker asked the priest not to disperse the scant forces of the earlier committee by creating a second one. "It creates a conflict, Father," he told the priest. "We are only a few."

The worker insisted but realizing his words were, as before, insufficient, he began to plead to no avail.

As he turned away, feeling hurt in his disappointment, he again tried for the last time to scrutinize the priest's eyes, setting aside the shame and guilt. He found out that even though the priest's love and concern for his people remained, the priest's innocence had already begun to disappear, dampening the glow of his youth.

What the worker found in place of the vanishing innocence was the dawning light of a new pride that might be transformed into the vain illusion of self-deceit, a strange light which from its nascent awakening was destined to blind the priest to his own self.

A feeling of certainty about the virtuous intent of his mission came over him while he walked, followed by members of the new committee amid the raucous noise of the crowd. And he was surprised to notice how his hand possessed a new self-confidence he had lacked before as he extended it to bless those who were kneeling, with a delicate but firm gesture that subtly commanded respect, an upward movement of the fingers which he now made a part of his blessing with extraordinary ease.

Many years later, in the waning days of the century of tragedies, several of the fearsome narco-traffickers who kept the whole continent in continuous stalemate, sprang from the barrio of the lowlands: children and grandchildren of those victimized by the resolution concerning public women.

XI
THE VIRGIN

WHEN SHE SAW THE PRIEST APPROACHING SHE thought he would surely rescue her from the taunts of the crowd, from these strange adult voices spoken with a malicious intonation, isolating her in a world she didn't understand. In the crowded street she looked like a lonely adolescent, a figure out of place, slow in her timidity, dressed humbly in a pauper's garments. Her face remained quiet, as if nothing disturbed her, and she pretended not to hear the talk about her small size, her insignificance, and her secret fears, insulting her and challenging her with vulgar sexual dares she had never heard before. Now that the priest was blessing her, as she knelt to receive that blessing, she waited in vain for him to realize she wasn't like the others who had come to the neighborhood; she waited in vain for him to know who she was: only a child who had lived her short life in the lowlands and that she wanted the mob to leave her alone, to stop pestering her. But when the priest approached in the street, blessed her and drew away without recognizing her urgent need, the adults around her resumed their efforts.

She was barefoot, and they told her that such a grown-up, beautiful woman like her needed a pair of red shoes for her dark little feet, to show off her legs when she danced. They laughed, looking at her slyly and amusing themselves at her expense. In spite of her youth and lack of experience with people outside the closely-knit circle of her family, she realized how this taunting was aimed at destroying her life. She read in the eyes of those who continued taunting her the tragic story of what her own life could become. She saw the destiny that waited inevitably for her if she surrendered her will to them, if she gave them what they were asking with their mocking, all-knowing eyes. She understood much better what they insinuated with their eyes than what they said with their words. She was still a fragile youngster, no longer a child but not yet a woman. The woman in her had not even begun to blossom. And as she got up to encounter those cunning and malicious looks, she heard one of the men say he wanted to caress her two little doves. He made a coarse gesture by putting his cupped hands on his chest so she would understand that the little doves had to do with her small breasts, although the real truth of what the demands meant escaped her. She was hungry, and they told her they knew where she could eat her fill. One of the women in the street made fun of her for receiving the blessing, for being so good, saying:

"You're no better than any of us."

Another woman came close and whispered coyly: "The lipstick you put on that pretty mouth already shows where you want to go. It betrays you. I'll take you and show you how to make a lot of money."

And one of the men, pretending to protect her, came to her side in the crowd and said in a mellifluous, seductive voice:

"I'll take good care of you, baby, and if you stick to me I'll protect you from anybody bothering you. You'll be safe with me."

Another man in an army uniform approached her and said: "I know a place around the corner where you can make a lot of money. I'll pay you well. You can count on money from me every week. You'll have enough to buy all the food and shoes and dresses you want."

"You've got only one chance to sell your innocence," another woman told her. "There is a place for little virgins like you. I can take you there if you give me a commission. The price would be good."

Some of the women told her they wished they could be young again, because the price of innocence was high; that life was short and she'd better take advantage; that there was a place for girls her age, a house for little greenhorn virgins where the city's rich men came to spend a fortune.

She looked around with anger, crying, pushing against those who came near her, who put their arms so close to her that they forced inescapable contact. Those insinuating voices pursuing her, all the vile talk and grotesque gestures disturbed and confused her. There, under the sun of this cloudless day, she was a sad, solitary figure surrounded by the crowd near her own home in the familiar neighborhood where she had lived her whole life among friends and which now appeared to be a foreign place in some unknown country on a planet different from her own. The truth suddenly came to her with terrifying insight, when she realized that her neighborhood had been transformed into a bleeding wound, into a grimace, an ancient ruin, and that everything she had known was gradually disappearing as if an apocalyptic flood were dragging everything toward an unfathomable pit.

After the priest disappeared none of the hundreds of faces around her, nor the events pressing upon her, seemed to fit the life she had known before. Even as she tried to remember how the streets used to look, streets that had been her childhood playground, the frenetic present intruded on her memories with an impact that destroyed all the past. What she saw were sweaty faces smiling tauntingly, pushy people drawing near her, the rows of tents in vacant lots, chairs and mattresses and scraps of paper and pillows moved by this mob in a strange, mad rush akin to a perverse nightmare that had nothing to do with the neighborhood of her innocent childhood games. Everything appeared strewn through the streets as if someone had played a bad joke of vandalistic proportions on those who lived there.

She had never seen so many people in one place. It seemed to her as if the whole city were there, jostling randomly in all directions, as if no one had anything better to do than loiter around the streets that had previously belonged to her.

Trying to find something unsoiled among the sweaty mess of lewdly dancing bodies, she looked up and saw the eternal blue of the sky like a promise she may yet strive for, telling her that no matter what the present conditions might be, she could still overcome the tragedy surrounding her. She realized that something very precious inside herself was rapidly changing as new events were unfolding around her with accelerated momentum. She was afraid for not feeling prepared for this change in the conditions surrounding her, made all the more difficult by the changes taking place in her own body, as it shifted from adolescence to womanhood. A part of her wanted to restore the peaceful protectiveness of old in spite of the poverty and hunger she had known there. But as she thought more deeply, she caught herself wishing for the death of all those who had come to disturb the peace of her beloved neighborhood.

She wanted to return to her home to hide. It was painful to feel so awkward, as if her hands and feet were too big for her small body. For the first time in her life she felt conscious of her body, now that she was being stared at by adults in ways she had never imagined.

She touched her mouth and felt the lipstick she had put on before leaving her house and blushed. Thinking of her parents, she wondered why they were so poor and why they lived in a neighborhood that was now being invaded by this frantic mob; why her family wasn't part of that group of wealthy people who lived in big houses protected by tall iron fences and with lawns and gardens around them. She felt an irreparable violation of her most intimate self; a feeling that had never been a part of her youth. She was horrified by her intense blushing and felt as if she were completely naked before the eyes of that rowdy mob, ruined and lost without recourse. A fear bordering on panic came over her when she thought that perhaps she would have to submit in order to continue living.

So broken and hurt, she couldn't stop crying, hating herself and all the others as well.

And then a torrent of despair and fury came over her as had once come over all the harlots who were now living in the street. Prolonged sobs began to twist her little face, shaking her fragile body with such intensity that those who surrounded her perhaps hearing in her lament the distant echoes of the agony of their misspent youth, became alarmed and suspended their cruel taunts, leaving her alone.

Taking advantage of this opportunity to escape, groping through the crowd for the way to the nearby chapel, blinded by tears as she was, the girl finally took flight from the mad rush of the senseless, sweaty swarm, searching for the calming protection of a familiar place where she sought to hide like a small, wounded animal.

No one followed her. They allowed her to pass and disappear from their lives as suddenly as she had appeared. They had used her as an object of ridicule and sport, remembering momentarily who they had been and what they might have succeeded in becoming when they were her same age. For a moment only, each felt the presence of a subtle shadow, intangible, indecipherable, which moved on. In an inexpressible but certain way each realized that the whirlwind of the life in which they were raised here in this city had finally submerged them in the depths of a barbarous anonymity that sealed their doom and condemned them to die long before closing their eyes for the last time.

But the sudden moment of awareness scurried away, a shadow of a passing cloud just real enough to turn their attention from the child who disappeared. No one thought of her again. She came and went out of their lives without leaving more than the flicker of a trace of momentary remorse.

When the child entered the chapel, she remained standing with her arms extended against the heavy portal, as if trying to create an unreachable wall between herself and the restless crowd that had outraged her modesty, knowing that in the struggle she had lost something ineffable which would forever mark her. She knew she would never forget those few minutes of confusion and anguish even if she managed to live for another hundred years.

Overwhelming waves of wrath besieged her. She wanted to scream but was afraid the noise would attract the crowd again. Only a muffled wail escaped her juvenile throat. She wanted to kick the door but only managed to strike the soles of her feet against the humid floor of that gloomy place which smelled of rot and incense, sweat, lime and the burnt tallow of candles which, as they did in her own home in the neighborhood, projected lights and shadows over the face of the statue of the Virgin near the altar.

She backed away suddenly and entered the flickering circle of light, grinding her teeth, feeling deceived and abused by the adult world which promised love and protection and ended up offering only poverty or slow death. What had happened to this body of hers? And what was this desire she harbored, this anxiety to be beautiful and grown-up, the urgency which made her feel detestable and which had nourished the harassing cries of ridicule and temptation in the wearying street?

She had never been so close to the Virgin before, even when her mother had brought her to pray in despair and deprivation through the long hungry days of her childhood, when they humbly prostrated themselves at her feet. This was the first time she had not knelt before the Virgin of her neighborhood's chapel. Here she was, standing instead; the two of them—the Virgin and her—face-to-face.

She stood right next to the unseeing eyes of the statue, smelling that gloomy odor, trying to divine an answer, some sign or revelation. It seemed strange to be here all alone, where she had come with her mother to pray for food, for their daily bread through the uncountable dawns of the deserted street that was barely illuminated by a streetlight and the quiver of stars already disappearing from the sky.

It was now, through a veil of tears, she saw for the first time the statue's face was broken, it wasn't perfect. The face had a small crack from the right temple, passed behind the ear, and ended down in her throat. The crack was almost concealed by a shadow but she could still see it clearly now that she was standing and their heads were at the same level.

The disillusion that had pursued men from the day they first carved gods in their own imperfect image seized the child. Had her innocence deceived her? Had the adults played another trick on her, another mocking joke? She touched her body with the palms of her open hands, slowly while she panted, as if trying to ascertain her most intimate identity, still sobbing. And the tormenting rage she had accumulated began to overflow, loosening an impetuous desire to do something prohibited which would transform everything and repair with a single magic act all the injustice and deceit she had suffered.

Her blood rushed inside her fragile body, her arteries transformed into immense rivers, filling her whole being with a violence that grasped her completely, making her spin around as if in a whirlwind, in frantic search for something solid with which to smash into a million crumbling pieces this statue of the pallid figure of a woman.

The statue which smiled distantly with her marble face, inscrutably hidden behind a veil of mystery and before which the child opened the most secret and protected corners of her heart so many times, where she promised in the name of all that was sacred and noble to live a saintly life, renouncing her unattainable and indomitable desires in exchange for a sign that would guide her, for some remote aid that would permit her to keep alive the hope of finding relief for herself, her parents, brothers and sisters, loomed before her. She would have sacrificed everything to fulfill her constant need to be received with love in some small, safe place where neither pain nor hunger would exist, where sickness was unknown, where the ungiving hand would never punish, where the wounding word would never be uttered.

Uncontrollable rage, the agony and blindness of fury, upset the balance of the girl's life, disrupting the necessary equilibrium which she maintained so precariously when the crowd had accosted her. And if in her anger she had had sufficient strength, everything around her would have been reduced to ashes, including her city and the cursed slums on the hills.

But when she couldn't find anything heavy to crush the statue, the pause slowed the vigor of her impulse and as she began to control her fury, she turned and found herself again face-to-face with the statue, like a savage who at last begins to understand the true perversity of an ancient enemy. And taking now from the pocket of her blouse a cheap old stick of lipstick which she had used only in secret to timidly adorn her lips, with the severe touches of the artist whose intent is to deform, she painted the cold and immutable mouth of the Virgin with the crimson color of lust.

She stood there a long time, sobbing, staring at the now painted face, as if surprised to discover how fear and rage had possessed her in such a manner, as she listened to the desperate wails coming from her own throat. But the wailing was contained as suddenly as it had begun, even though her tears continued falling in silence. The weary struggle in her heart she longed to express in a lament to drown all the insults uttered against her finally abated, but she couldn't stop the desire that saddened her so and which could be calmed only by love and freedom.

The child realized how helpless she was, knew she possessed scant forces to confront the terrors waiting outside in a world with which she would have to contend the rest of her life. She didn't know where she would find the courage or the wisdom to struggle in such a contradictory world, a world whose cruelty she didn't create; or how she would acquire the courage to rise above adversity, instead of allowing herself to be dragged into the morass of prostitution. She wanted to become something noble and worthy, to triumph as a teacher in some school like the one from which she was ejected, or to become a nurse in a hospital for the poor like those she had always known in the country she loved so much and which belonged to all of them, or to do whatever task would give her self-respect.

She looked wearily around her. As she recognized all the familiar paintings of saints and demons, the crosses with their shadows that languished throughout the humid chapel, the awful paleness of that woman with the mysterious veil and the hateful crack and the red, deformed lips looking now similar to the outrageous lips of the women who had invaded the tranquillity of her neighborhood; as she perceived the ruin of the crucified figure that bled on the altar, she felt more alone than she had ever felt in her short life, as if everything around her were distant and foreign, as if all had changed completely and irrevocably.

She dried her tears, knowing with certainty that the years of her childhood were gone and that the child who had entered the chapel no longer existed.

Slowly, without crying, she opened the heavy inner portal and went out into the street. No one noticed her. She walked down the street among the restless crowd with a firm step, looking for a road out of the darkness and terror surrounding her.

XII
THE SEARCH

THE IRON HAND OF TYRANNY FORCED OPEN THE doors of the neighborhood, allowing entrance to arrogant speculators who scorned the protests and the pleas of the occupants. Those who came to fatten themselves on the people's weakness haughtily inspected each house, asking unanswerable questions, grudgingly appraising the homes, converting them into contemptible commercial objects, and finally making wretched offers at a public auction presided over by an insolent group of officials who tried to lend an appearance of legality to the swindles, pretending they were urgent transactions consistent with the great constitutional right and democratic privilege of buying and selling for what was ostensibly called a free and open market.

The bidders were mostly monied pimps whose intention was to establish bordellos in the neighborhood, in shameless, barely hidden complicity with the government auctioneers. They began with insignificant offers which remained at confiscatory levels, knowing that the small print in the new laws would favor their battle against neighborhood home owners.

Often those who became buyers were the auctioneers who had forced the residents to sell by means of legalistic tricks and under penalty of losing all their possessions or a detention whose length was undetermined. The more the residents resisted, the less they were offered.

So it came to pass that houses constructed through years of manual labor, built with the sweat of the occupants and costing the lifelong efforts of several generations, raised piece by piece with all the initiative of the human spirit, were now snatched away by the irony of a law imposed by the powerful and put into effect by corrupt executors.

Come what may, each confiscated fragment of those homes would remain inextricably linked to the most intimate and common desires of the working class neighborhood residents, anchored in their blood, going back to parents and grandparents, touching the deepest feelings of all who had lived there; each piece a living memorial recounting the history of its existence on earth and which now, in the midst of that hysterical and bewildering struggle, cried out aimlessly in the confusion of the terrible, ironic action with a thundering vehemence that bordered on delirium and that at times screamed in a silent language understood only by a few.

"That floor tile broke the day my first son was born!"

"We installed this roof beam the night before our daughter's marriage."

"Here's the window where my father looked out for the last time just before he died."

"Over there, the door we stole the night of the big typhoid epidemic."

And now, the door and the window, the broken floor tile and the roof beam—all would be uprooted and snatched from the beating heart, driven from the flesh and bones, destroying the cherished memory, tearing out what was still uneaten between the hungry jaws, what was almost within reach of the avid hands which would never quite possess what they longed for, trembling with passion, fear and anger, just as it always had happened.

The fathers of the families who rebelled and refused to sell their houses disappeared as if the earth had swallowed them. When a committee of neighbors managed to organize a public demonstration, it was immediately broken by the military forces, and the leaders were incarcerated. Those who survived were tortured until they promised to conform to the conditions imposed by the recent government decrees. Finally, when the women and children, against whom the officials initially didn't want to use their brutal methods, refused to leave their homes, they were carried screaming to the middle of the streets and dumped like sacks of produce among the furniture, bedclothes and cooking utensils which had been ejected in reckless disorder from the defenseless homes.

There, in their neighborhood street, they were dispossessed and abandoned to their fate among the storm of insults and lawlessness, each one forced to fend alone, the majority obliged to exchange their meager possessions for hardly enough to subsist on, thrown out from their homes among the ravenous mob to eventually be gobbled up by the inhuman tide, disappearing and losing touch with one another like flotsam in the whirl of disaster.

In vain they searched the street for protection by a law that existed only to destroy them, trusting still in the miracle that liars had inculcated in them all through their childhoods, still waiting for a change that refused to take place in a deaf country unwilling to condescend to their needs, praying nevertheless for the triumph of one of their sons in the Senate of the Republic, one who wouldn't betray them in his rise to prominence, one who would remember his own childhood in the slums, who would not sell out to the powerful and who would rescue them from martyrdom.

They looked on with sinking hearts at the failure of their efforts, finally giving the children part of their dwindling possessions, telling them to get away, to escape to the provinces and join distant relatives who might care for them, far from this living hell. The majority of the homes already flaunted the bloody lights of lechery, converted into houses of prostitution. Only a few structures remained in the silence of darkness and isolation, pitifully adorned with a few religious relics—crosses, statues of Christ and the Virgin—which the residents displayed like talismans, thinking their presence would defend them against the sexual fervor that ran amuck insatiably through the streets, thinking that the icons would protect them from the public's assault.

For an eternity they patiently awaited the return of their absent men, those who had disappeared after they protested, those who were prisoners of the hated authorities. The women suspected their men were dead but refused to give up hope or their desecrated neighborhood. Some waited until they were obliged to exchange everything they owned for food and medicines. And when nothing remained, some of the younger mothers and the adolescent girls—trapped and hungry—felt in their despair that their only resource was to join the enslaved women of the brothels in what had once been their homes. Gone were the undying dreams of freedom where they had known the serenity of a transitory peace in a past now almost forgotten in the midst of these incredible and bewildering events, even yet hoping for the return of their protectors, trying to hold onto a bit of what had been wrested so cruelly from them.

Others carried away what they could to the provinces, leaving a trail of messages and small objects that would serve as a sign for the absent lover, for the vanished father, always hoping these men would be found in some distant future. And many of the women and children returned to the filthy shanty towns on the mountainsides around the city where they were born, to take up again a beggar's existence. But a few stayed in their old homes until the end. Among them was a woman whose husband was one of the principal organizers of the public demonstrations.

The soldiers found her dying and carried her in her bed to the middle of the street among the other unfortunates. Her son, who was no more than twelve years old, with the wild look of an animal trapped by superior forces, grabbed her nearly rigid hand desperately, clinging to the bed while those strange uniformed men moved it. He didn't speak, but once in a while raised his black eyes and his look probed the souls of those who were destroying his home. And those startled, disturbed eyes, that intense and deliberate stare, recorded every scene, each gesture, memorized every act, to etch all the features of his tormentors in his mind, to record those images and convert them into non-erasable memories which he would carry and evoke instantly until the end of the long days of a life which he now thought he would dedicate exclusively to the unequal struggle against injustice. His gaze passed from soldier to soldier, almost calmly now that he was resigned to the worst, studying the unmoving faces, the discolored uniforms, the heavy boots, the bayonets reflecting a thousand needles of sunlight.

He couldn't understand how it was possible that other men, similar to his own father and to himself, who used the same words he used, men who were also born in poverty and who knew well the hard life of hunger, could abuse him and dispossess him of the little his parents owned, could become persecutors of their own people. Maybe they would desist in this ill-fated determination and would ask his forgiveness for the outrages committed and tell him they would return his father, assure him that his dying mother would yet have her moment of peace. Inexplicably and for only a few moments the consoling idea occurred to him that there was even time for them to make restitution, that the soldiers had the power to undo the evil they had created and that they would restore the placid existence the boy had known in his neighborhood. They were his countrymen and they should understand. But they implacably continued to follow the orders of their commander, ignoring the boy, as if his moans and puzzled, accusing look were only minor, passing obstructions in their routine.

He remembered then what his father had told him so many times:

"The hungry sons of the oppressed frequently serve their tormentors by putting on the uniform of an army of slaves in exchange for a crust of bread or for the promise of a future without the constant fear of grinding poverty. And because of their desire to be numbered among the dominant of their kind. It is their way to feel they belong among the powerful."

He looked at the soldiers again, and when he convinced himself for certain that these men were indeed those same uniformed puppets of whom his father had spoken, when he confirmed without a doubt that those men were the sellouts who carried out the orders of his father's enemies, he raised his voice against them with an unfamiliar strength that came from a source until then unknown to him.

"Someday I'll kill all of you," he said simply, as if speaking of something that had already happened.

The soldiers were surprised to hear such a threat from the mouth of a child who appeared so weak, and they looked at him with open mouths, momentarily stunned and not knowing how to reply.

A gentle breeze moving down from the mountains caressed their faces. But the men didn't realize it was the promise of liberty which perfumed the mountain ranges of their country. Only the boy sensed its meaning; only he breathed in the essence of the land that belonged to him. The soldiers heard the boy's threat and felt, after the brief refreshing moment of the almost imperceptible breeze, the foreboding shadow of death revealed in those few childish words. A slight feeling of anxiety, almost unconscious, confused them while their eyes blinked. And trying to forget those challenging words, they began to bow their heads while they laughed, as a sign of exaggerated respect that was the quintessence of mockery, clutching their rifles uneasily nevertheless, pretending to have more fear than they were sensitive enough to sense in themselves, not daring to look inside their own souls, and saying finally to each other:

"This little pest of a mad boy is sure wild."

"Yeah, watch out; *tiene bolas muy grandes*, he's got very big balls."

"If we let our guard down this little stud *nos come vivos*, will eat us alive."

"Sure he's got balls!"

"He might mount you any minute, ha, ha, ha!"

They laughed but their hands held firmly on to their rifles.

But the boy heard only his mother's broken voice calling him urgently, and he felt the fever in the delicate hand touching him and her fear on seeing in him the same rebelliousness that had tormented her husband, that profound rebelliousness he had held inside through many long years of outrage and humiliation and which had burst out that day when at the head of the neighborhood workers' demonstration he was detained and mercilessly beaten, when they dragged him defeated and unconscious at the end of that terrible day of strife, along with his many comrades, into oblivion.

Now the mother embraced her son and begged him not to hate. She drew him down to her until her lips could murmur in his ear:

"Escape! Look for your father and escape because hatred and violence will trap you and ruin you, my son."

And having spoken those words, with great effort she raised her arm and blessed him as was her custom whenever they parted even for very short periods of time, already closing her eyes to withdraw into death's final silence.

When a cart pulled by a gray mule arrived to carry his mother away, the soldiers cordoned off the place so no one would come to ask embarrassing questions. They put her in a box of cheap planks then placed the box on top of a two-wheeled cart. The boy followed, unnoticed, across his neighborhood toward unfamiliar streets, crossing the river by a bridge whose rusty metal supports squeaked at each step of the mule, as they headed to the paupers' cemetery hill. And before the sun of that beautiful spring day sank, he saw the driver unload the wooden box, specter of an improvised coffin barely large enough to contain his mother's broken remains, and drag it toward one of the many holes that patiently awaited inhabitants. The driver slid the box into the open grave and using a shovel, covered it with earth. Then the man brought over two pieces of wood he tied together in the form of a cross and unceremoniously sunk it in the fresh dirt, finally going away in the cart, sweating copiously but pleased with himself for having performed something beyond the call of duty.

When the boy was alone and sure no one would see him, he slowly approached the grave where his mother was buried. He stopped there as if on the edge of an abyss whose depths he tried to fathom with his penetrating look, without the capacity to understand what he saw: a mound of dirt with two sticks tied together in the form of a cross on top. Under the mound and the make-shift cross he knew his mother lay inside the wooden box. And he wondered how it was possible that barely a few hours before, his mother had caressed his hand and told him not to hate.

Now it seemed everything happening was part of something outside his own life, as if his present life belonged to someone else, to some unfortunate orphan unknown to him.

The shadows lengthened.

The boy thought about finding his father, the only person left to him, in order to carry out his mother's last wishes. Perhaps he could regain the happy dream of hope, that dream of which his father had spoken so many times. It was difficult to concentrate his gaze and his thoughts on this plot of earth, impossible to accept his fate.

"Now you're buried in the wooden box," he repeated several times, as if trying to convince himself. "And I will never see you again."

He thought about digging her up. But he stopped, realizing he could not change the reality of his mother's death and recover the peace his family had known in their home.

It was a truth he had to accept: everything he had known and trusted was changed completely as if some satanic power had turned all the cosmic forces upside down.

"There's nothing, there's nothing, there's nothing I can do," he said as if speaking to her.

He raised his eyes and looked toward the big city in the valley, automatically searching in the distance for his neighborhood, hoping to find something familiar, but he only saw rows of strange houses like remote little toys in a movie set, houses with red adobe roofs, indistinct spots that disappeared with the last rays of the sun and the approaching darkness.

He felt an air of calm that evening, a feeling that contradicted everything happening to him. The calm helped him surrender to the weariness that overcame him, as if the life of the valley had regenerated itself into a beautiful promise, as if the arrogance and greed of those men he hated were impotent before the indestructible splendor of the evening now sinking into darkness.

Looking toward the city below and the surrounding mountains, it seemed to the boy that something ineffable and lasting out there belonged to him forever, and this spectacle mitigated the pain oppressing him.

He felt less pursued by the terror spread by evil men and began to sense the quiet solitude of this desolate cemetery as he contemplated the immortality of the mountains and the valley and felt the proximity of the inevitable night.

He was overcome by a feeling of strength more ancient than his young age could grant and was finally able to cry in great waves of sobbing while pounding his small fists on the earth where his lifeless mother rested. Night fell and the child continued crying silently until he fell into a deep sleep as he had done many times before, hungry in his mother's arms. But now, in exhaustion, all he embraced were the still warm clods of earth and all that covered him was a blanket of nocturnal darkness.

The first rays of the morning sun that barely penetrated the darkness from the other side of the mountains woke him suddenly. He didn't remember where he was and for a moment expected to find the world around him as it had always been. But then he saw the wooden cross in front of his sleepy eyes and realized his hands still held the clods of earth. When the traces of death confronted him, all the tragic events of the previous day flooded his memory again, overwhelming him. As soon as he moved his eyes he felt tired again, overcome by a terrible weight.

"Now I must search all the hidden corners of the city to find my father, to carry out the promise I made to my mother, her last wish," he mumbled.

Shaking off the dust covering his body he gradually moved toward the cross on the grave, extending his hand until he touched it tenderly. Then he got up and searched among the other tombs marked with unfamiliar names. And after a futile search he slowly moved away, already looking anxiously toward the valley, turning his back on the cemetery, not wanting to look again at what had served as his bed the night before. He saw the river's bluish thread piercing and then losing itself in a thick veil of clouds in the distance and set off downhill without even the slightest of backward glances. His steps were deliberate, as if to conserve his strength now that he would need all his energy to look throughout the confines of the city, searching from one side of the valley to the other, by the outlying neighborhoods and where the river formed the enormous swamps which were a frequent refuge of those who were running from the law.

Wherever he went he inquired about his father's whereabouts. The response was always doubtful: "Maybe you'll find him at the prison." "Perhaps he escaped to the provinces." Some of the people knew the father because of his activities in the neighborhood committee and they drew away from the boy when they saw him, protecting him from their suspicions and fearful that the authorities would accuse them of aiding the son of an enemy. For what beside torture and death could the weak expect at the hands of the powerful against whose laws they rebelled? And how were they to talk about such suspicions with a pleading child? Realizing they were going away in silence, that they were avoiding him, the boy continued to pester them, hurrying his steps with a desperate urgency, as if he had a presentiment that his father was in imminent danger and that he might be the only one to save him. It was still morning when he walked by the walls outside the prison, moving faster as he went along, putting aside his tiredness.

He remembered how his father told him this was the prison where they put the poor who couldn't pay a lawyer to defend them.

The boy stopped next to the main gate which was guarded by police armed with machine guns. When he asked the guards about his father they told him to wait a while for the return of the criminals who worked in the night shift on the highways and were due anytime. He watched the long lines of prisoners—

wretched pariahs in their own country—returning in chains from the long day of forced labor. He called out for his father by name and described him to those who would listen. All the stooped men, bound to each other, marched silently after the long night's work, worn out by the odious hours of unpaid labor, carrying their heavy tools. But the child didn't give up and continued hounding everyone he saw until one of the men said impatiently:

"You might find him under the city."

The child cried in anguish upon hearing the man's utterance. He had heard how the officials disposed of their enemies, torturing them first and afterwards hurling them still alive but defenseless—bound by their hands and feet— into the stinking sewers that ran below the city, there to die a hopeless and painful death.

He drew away in fear, refusing to search among the dead but obsessed by the idea of his father dying alone in the darkness under the city. He took off running, not wanting to hear those words, and resumed his task of inquiring through the thousand streets, calling his father's name, looking in places where the poor often ended their lives.

"Where do they take the poor when they die?"

The answers he received led him first to the city's jails, the military barracks, to the storehouse for unclaimed bodies and the medical school's dissection laboratories where the children of the illustrious owners of the republic studied anatomy on the mutilated bodies of the humble in order to cure the powerful while the poor died for lack of medical care.

He found no trace of his father. The people he asked either didn't know or didn't want to tell him. But he continued running through avenues he had never seen before, where beautiful gardens and mansions were well-guarded by high iron fences. And briefly he saw what a carefree life would be like in his own city, comfortable and easy, which neither his father nor his ancestors had enjoyed, having known only the arduous fatigue that produced barely enough to buy daily crusts of bread.

All afternoon he ran with urgent speed from one side of the city to the other, stopping from time to time to ask about his father until he found himself again in his old neighborhood in the valley's lowlands next to the swamps and again encountered the same savage music and confusion that had destroyed his home. He felt like an old man who returns to the scenes of his youth to find everything uprooted and irrevocably altered.

The evening of his long, exhausting day came and the image of his father suffocating beneath the city pursued him. He climbed the hills to look in the caves and shacks of tin and cardboard. But he obtained no answers to his questions and wandered erratically in big circles through the immense slums, running into the same people he had questioned earlier until he fell exhausted by hunger and fatigue into the arms of a humble family who gave him food and a corner to rest.

He slept through the night until noon of the next day. He was awakened by an old blind woman who shook him gently and said: "You'll find him under the city. Here's a candle and matches to guide you. Look for him in the outlet of the sewer next to the main army barracks." Then she fed him well but, in answer to his many insistent questions, all she said was, "I told you: go into the sewers by the outlet closest to the main army barracks. Tie this bag of sweet smelling herbs around your face to overcome the stench."

On this, the third day of his ordeal, the child ran down the hill gripping the candle, with the matches and bag of herbs in his pocket, fearing to look in the direction of the numerous sewer inlets. Knowing he eventually would have to find the courage and subdue his fear of entering the filthy current of the city's main sewer, he looked now into one of the small inlets in the suburbs to test his valor.

He walked a few steps into the inlet until darkness and stench made him stop. It made him furious to realize he wasn't yet capable of descending farther into the dark where unknown dangers might lurk among the living secrets of the black, moldy rocks, the place where the small streams were dammed up, walled in, trapped in the subterranean bed where he might find his father.

He withdrew with repugnance, holding his breath until he again found himself at a safe distance, where he didn't feel the nauseating gusts of rotten dampness, knowing that only death and decomposition lay in wait in the bowels of the city. He felt frustrated by his own cowardice. It seemed to him as if he had walked in search of his father for years and that he would never find him.

He walked out of the inlet toward the army barracks designated by the blind woman, where the river that crossed the city was channeled and the many small creeks and sewer outlets met. As he walked, he stopped to look at the drains suspiciously, inspecting the tunnels. Here, as he approached the barracks, they were more accessible.

For a long time he prowled around the inlet the blind woman of the hills had indicated, watching the soldiers who lounged beside the barracks, not daring to approach the gap for fear of being caught. But as he remembered the words of the old woman and the prisoners in chains, he gradually surmounted his fear, thinking that perhaps his father was wounded and in need of help in the depths of those tunnels.

He sat by the edge of the inlet, playing with a small stone in case the soldiers were observing him. But the sight of a boy in rags loitering was not unusual and the soldiers didn't even notice.

Approaching the edge of the opening he peered into the impenetrable darkness beyond and suddenly heard what he perceived as a distant moan, like that of a man in pain. He didn't think again of the dangers awaiting him, nor of the hidden mysteries he feared lay in ambush among the formless shadows he could vaguely discern. He finally plunged beyond the veiled threshold into the twilight vapors. He walked upstream, against the fetid current without knowing where he was going, groping along the damp walls until his hands began to bleed, hurt by the piercing rocks he touched to guide himself.

He stopped walking as he sensed the walls were narrowing, the sharp stones becoming increasingly wounding. It was now safe to light the candle. Its light would not be detected by any peering soldier who might have become suspicious. As soon as the candle was lit and moved searchingly from side to side, the boy's shadow became gigantic, trembling abruptly in the flickering light, extending itself at times to the walls and ceilings of the caves in the distance.

It seemed to the boy that figures of death were spying on him from their resting places among the dark rocks. He listened intently, without hearing what he had previously thought was a human moan, but heard only the constant flow of the water eating away at the entrails of the city throbbing above. He paused again and took out the bag of sweet smelling herbs dangling on a long string and tied it around his face so the bag covered his nose. He took a deep breath to enjoy the clean smell of the herbs, their sweet and minty odor. He felt comforted and smiled, remembering the good breakfast the poor family had provided for him, the comfortable mattress he slept on. He smiled gratefully and vowed to someday give them money they deserved, if he ever had enough.

"All I have are rags, a candle, some matches, a bag of herbs on a string and a stomach full of good food. Most of my riches are gifts from them," he whispered to himself as in a reverie.

When he ventured into one of the smaller tunnels he bumped into a man's lifeless body. He examined the body under the tremulous light, trying to recognize him, but he could barely make out the vestiges of a face half-eaten by worms. As soon as he touched the face to see if it was his father's and saw the horrible sight, he drew back with repugnance. Could that be his father? No! A thousand times no! His father's face was vigorous! His father's eyes were not empty, they looked toward the skies of his homeland with pride and with the longing of a man who loved it, a man who was respected by those who knew him as a leader of his working comrades. Those vacuous bits of flesh still lingering in the sockets could neither see nor did they reflect the least trace of free will.

He withdrew, clambering hurriedly on all fours, fearing to look back.

He found a tunnel so narrow he barely fit inside. A few steps after entering the opening the fetid slime under his feet turned thicker and began to rise to his knees. And then he again heard another moan and recklessly rushed headlong toward a dark figure that was splashing spasmodically in the mire and which on examination turned out to be a man bound hand and foot with a huge slash in his throat out of which his tongue had been pulled by some barbarian who left it to hang limply, leaving the terrifying impression of an anatomical anomaly resembling a festive bow tie where the tongue stuck out and the blood flowed.

He recognized it instantly as "the bow tie cut" that people dreaded and that he had heard many talk about with fear. But as soon as he drew closer to look at what his eyes had never seen before, what he could never imagine could happen, once he perceived what he thought was an insane vision, he drew back screaming, thinking for a moment that it was his father and began to vomit at the same time. The man continued moaning incoherently and suddenly his eyes glazed over as if a coat of ice had suddenly formed there and his body sank into the awful filth.

No! His father was taller! His father would never die like this! The child shook his head as if wanting to rid himself of the image he had beheld and left the man to sink in the mud.

He began to run toward one of the other tunnels, having great difficulty moving, the sticking substance he walked on growing deeper with each step. He shouted his father's name in terror and stopped to listen intently to the fading reverberations of his own clamor as it returned to him in the form of a pursuing echo bouncing off the vile walls.

As he struggled to move on, he slipped and fell like the man with the terrible wound. He hauled himself upright, shaking the scum off his own body, trembling with fear, rage and revulsion on contact with the rottenness, with the repugnant thickness of fecal matter running through the sickening bog, hating those who were responsible for these atrocious apparitions and who walked with impunity above these sewers in the city streets. In his bewilderment, the light from his candle went out, but he didn't pause to light it again now that he wanted to get out of this tunnel as quickly as possible and escape from seeing the man who died in his presence.

He found himself lost in the darkness, bumping against the walls of the labyrinths, slipping now and then and falling into the foulness, running into dead-end tunnels, crying and shouting angrily against the soldiers and all the rest of the unknown powerful men who had brought him to his present state.

He began to run as much as the viscosity of the liquids surrounding him allowed, in spite of the tremendous difficulty he had moving, until he arrived at a wider tunnel. He felt the freshness of an unpolluted spring where he rested and washed. Upon catching his breath he lit the candle again after several matches went out in his trembling hands.

Resting there on the damp soil next to the small stream he wondered in astonishment where he was, wandering beneath the city. He pondered on his fate and listened acutely to a faint murmur, like a secret whisper, as if someone were calling him by name from one of the narrowest tunnels. Suddenly his heart skipped a savage beat and a cold feeling akin to ice invaded his stomach, forcing from him a few faltering cries that were the uncontrollable sounds of terror. He wanted to hide, to vanish forever, because he was sure it was his father's voice and he was afraid to see him in agony, to discover lacerations on the loved body he could not restore to health, to witness his pain and humiliation. But then he thought if that be the case, if his father were to die in his arms, hadn't that been part of his mission? Wasn't it part of the promise he had made to his dying mother? Could he live with himself if now, at the last moment, he would recoil from his mission? And what if there might be a chance to save him?

He answered the call, softly at first, and when he received no answer, shouted without restraint. But when the last echo of his wild screams vanished in those endless and intricate labyrinths and the sepulchral silence engulfed him once again, he didn't hesitate and went toward the unknown source of the whispered name with a fury and determination he never suspected he could muster.

The boy ran into the bodies of two men whose

faces he examined under the flickering candlelight. They were dressed in uniforms he didn't recognize, still grotesquely wearing their caps. Only their skeletons remained. Then he saw others in various stages of decomposition, some exhibiting brutal gashes. Two bodies seemed fresher. They were next to each other, lying by a stream. When he touched them, they moved, filling him with fear and expectation, hoping he might yet find and save his father. He looked at them but didn't recognize them. No, they were not alive. They had only moved because he had changed their positions. Nothing could survive in this hell. He saw other bodies lying stiffly. He began to poke around in the mud, trying to see the faces without being able to tell if they were alive or dead. He moved from one to the other, getting confused. But none of them looked like his father! Those inert bodies without a vestige of life in them could never be like him. Those that appeared to him to be still alive had neither the strength nor the tenderness nor the intensity, nor anything he could remember about his father.

At the end of his search it seemed as if an even darker shadow had settled over him. Yes, some of those moans he had heard had sounded like his name, but he wasn't sure if his overwrought imagination conjured up such sounds. It was very confusing because the bodies made a gurgling in the mud as they slid into it. He wondered who beside his father could call on him, know his name. Or had he been mistaken? Was it only his deepest wish to have the man he loved so much call him by his name once again, to hear the strong voice of his beloved father for the last time?

He looked again, as if trying to recapture something elusive, feeling insensitive now after seeing the remains of another world, a strange place he had never suspected could exist so close to the familiar streets above. He stuck the candle into the mud by the side of a stream to pause. He closed his eyes and held his head in his hands. He knew he had run out of tears, that he would, in all likelihood, never cry again in his life. Bending down he looked with great intensity at one of the dead bodies surrounding him. His stature was like that of his father's. He brought the dead face next to his. How many of those faces had he examined? How long was he lost since he entered the tunnels?

Even though the odor of human waste sickened him, and he was crushed by the magnitude of what was happening, he sat in a niche of the wall, unable to cry, wondering if it wouldn't be easier to die here among his elders than have to go on living with those bizarre images engraved on his memory for the rest of his life. Suddenly, the unfathomable feelings beyond his grasp crystallized into a memory of the ancient tale his father often told about how an entire tribe of his ancestors preferred to die rather than be enslaved.

The tribe had hanged themselves from the tree branches of a distant mountain forest beside a lake many years ago, when the white conquerors first appeared in their country. Now he wondered how many boys like him had searched among those trees for their parents. Thinking about it that way, he supposed he wasn't the first nor the last to be lost among the dead. For a moment the thought served to bring him a small measure of consolation.

The light of his candle was slowly fading. But he was no longer afraid. His heart felt numb. He thought again about how he had lost his way. Soon it would be night again. But he was sure he could find his way out if he followed the movement of the waters. Time had lost its meaning and he paused to think what he would do once he found his way out of the sewer. He could see only three paths before him, three possibilities: emulate his father and the man his father had most admired, the one who was in the Senate and defended the rights of the poor—but such a path was mainly closed to people like himself and he doubted he could overcome all the difficulties those in power would place in his way. It was only a vague thought.

Two, he could join the guerrillas who were eager to enlist children to serve as messengers no one suspected, but who were later given more responsibilities, returning the terror doled out by the powerful ones. He would enjoy fighting against the bastards who had destroyed his family.

Third, he could serve as a mule, the name they gave to those who carried drugs in the burgeoning traffic beginning to enrich some of the poor. Later, if he could prove himself and save enough of what he'd make running the errands, he might buy and sell the coca and other drugs whose names he didn't even know and thus become very wealthy, while turning his tormentors into helpless addicts. All the poor talked about it as a way out of their humiliating poverty. He knew his father had been tempted but had refused to follow such a path for it was dangerous and led to crime.

He thought again about his father.

Attempting to put an end to his self-absorption, the boy tried to evoke his father's image, to recapture the memory of his father's face or some physical feature that might serve as a starting point, a base upon which he might construct his own existence. He was astonished to discover that, in spite of his focused effort, his mind wasn't able to shape the least trace of his father's face or body. The beloved image had vanished. He would have to conjure up a father of his own.

Renewing his effort to remember some happy occasion from the past when he used to play with his father, when he listened intently to the many tales his father told, and above all to a message his father spoke about human rights when he painted with skillful words what his country would become some day, his thoughts shifted before he could focus the longed-for memory of the physical aspects of his father. Only the feeling remained.

That strong, proud man who taught him the immortal dream would remain forever submerged in this obscurity of oblivion. But the child knew the vision of promise by heart and he repeated it now, first like a prayer and then shouting it like a defiant challenge: "The poor also have rights!"

For a long time he walked among the debris trying to find the light of day, no longer calling his father's name.

He followed the course of the descending water, certain he would arrive at the main river's outflow. Pausing from time to time, touching the walls, he heard the muffled rubbing of the slow but constant and implacable erosion of the city's foundations: the corruption wearing away at the structure surrounding him, sliding through the walls of the excavations and carrying in its subtle friction little pieces of sand and smaller pebbles that slowly fell in the slippery mud of the sewers around him.

He heard thousands of bubbles bursting, the sound of rats running around him, their gnawing as they consumed the city's garbage, and the continuous flux of the foul waters corroding the massive structures of the city's foundations.

He listened intently, almost forgetting he was lost in the semi-darkness, the light of his candle flickering the last dim vestiges of light, as if he were bewitched, immersed in his own exhaustion, without knowing where he was.

He was suddenly startled by the vigorous sound of the solemn, monotonous tolling of the iron bells whose deep tones floated through the subterranean passageways and caused the shadows to tremble. But instead of being afraid, he looked upward with a grotesque grimace on his tortured, childish face, as if revealing a blurred, victorious smile. And at the instant when he looked up toward the filthy roof, he knew with certainty that he was in the very heart of the city, below the great metropolitan cathedral.

FIFTH PART

XIII
THE REVOLUTION

WHEN THE LOST CHILD EMERGED FROM THE subterranean labyrinth, his dazed eyes still reflected the shadows of a dead world. But those who saw him come out of the sewers by the cathedral, all bloody and covered with filth, an obdurate figure that appeared to have been engaged in an uneven battle against the elements, would remember the moment, not only because the improbable image of the infuriated child was so brutal, but because the memory would fit the totality of violence that burst out in the city with a staggering and devastating force that would change the course of the nation's history.

The howls of defiance exploding from the youthful throat were fused with the shouts of rebellion and fury which burst out throughout the city and spread across the entire republic within minutes.

Some day in the distant future historians would write books about the events of that day so urgently transmitted over the radio and television in news bulletins that interrupted the usual daily programs:

"The main defender of the country's underdogs in the Senate of the Republic, the spokesman for the unfortunate who emerged from poverty and never forgot his origins, a man who became the representative of his people, who succeeded in surviving hundreds of political battles and imprisonment for his ideals until he became the titular head of his party and the most likely candidate for the presidency in the coming elections, was shot down on the steps of the Senate where for many years he was considered the wisest and most incorruptible representative of the people. It is not known for certain yet, for there's much confusion surrounding the assassination attempt, whether he is still alive or not, but it is feared his death would cause widespread violent revolutionary demonstrations throughout the country. The assailant, after shooting the revered leader pointblank, ran away and is still hiding behind the metal grating of a pharmacy on the other side of the plaza across from the Senate building, held at bay by an enraged crowd."

The great leader died after a few minutes of agony and news of the tragic events spread throughout the country like wildfire, with information pouring out even as the happenings were unfolding from moment to moment, with newscasters reporting from the scene.

After his death was announced an uneasy calm, that often precedes a storm, reflected a momentary state of utter confusion. Upon hearing the overwhelming news and the recounting of the victim's life transmitted frenziedly by the radio and television stations from the very place where the national calamity had taken place, before mass communications were plunged into silence by official censorship, it was feared that even more oppressive measures would begin to pave the way for general strikes and civil disobedience. It was widely feared that such open confrontations with the authorities would inevitably lead the country toward civil war.

But before the lines of communication were cut, the following dispatch was heard in every city, village and hamlet, in a voice that was barely able to conceal the excruciating pain felt by the reporter:

"The great leader who now lies dead had sworn to liberate the poor people of his country. He was one of them, well acquainted with the daily tyranny and violence experienced by the underprivileged classes: he had sold newspapers throughout his childhood and shined shoes during his adolescent years in the city's streets and taverns in order to survive and help his impoverished family.

Endowed with a superior intelligence and sensibility, he was capable of continuing his studies in spite of grave adversities, becoming at an early age his family's sole supporter. Since his earliest days in the city's slums he had kept alive his ambition to represent the working class, which he succeeded in doing as one of the youngest senators. He held that position for many years, using the existing laws to help the oppressed and patiently forging opportunities to become the head of his political party, a position he succeeded in gaining a few months ago, before he was designated as a candidate for the presidency.

"He was responsible for the most socially-oriented legislation the country had ever known. Among the laws he helped create are the increase in minimum wage, national health benefits and housing for destitute people, unemployment protection, broad expansion of educational opportunities for workers, and many other legislations. His numerous political enemies among the wealthy classes—'the lords of commerce and industry' as he called them— who had vainly tried to bribe him, swore to depose him from office resorting to any means available. However, until now, his extraordinary political astuteness and his enormous popularity among workers kept him beyond their reach. Jailed on trumped-up charges on several occasions by his detractors, he always managed to land on his feet and outsmart them at every turn, causing by his very cleverness enormous antagonism and hatred that often bordered on irrationality.

"The leader now dead always believed social and economic reforms must be carried out through the proper channels established by constitutional laws, refusing to take part in armed revolts against the regime though steadfastly maintaining the position of being its most assiduous critic.

"He was the first person from the po orest strata of our society since the nation was founded five hundred years ago to rise to power, often risking his life for causes no one else dared take up in thousands of parliamentary debates, tempting nevertheless in each encounter the idle hands of those who wished to snatch away the unselfish life that finally was brought to an end by the criminal barrage of traitorous bullets.

"Those who saw him die only a few minutes ago say that in the last moments of his life he regretted not having followed a more openly revolutionary course of action and urged those present to carry out a general strike that would paralyze the entire nation, saying that the workers and peasants should defend their rights by force or they would be subjugated for another century.

"The hopes he fomented over so many years of work now lie with the remains of his dead body, surrounded already by thousands of people who loved him and who cannot believe that their candidate, their beloved defender, could be dead and that his voice is stilled forever by those who...."

At that moment all communication wires were disconnected, and the country was isolated from the rest of the world. Troops began to occupy the radio and TV stations, the newspapers opposed to the regime were taken over by the military forces, and all newscasts and publications ceased. Later in the day, nothing was heard over the radio except the smooth rhythm of boleros with refrains about prohibited and impossible loves, and the television stations presented only insipid telenovellas.

Those who found themselves near the victim tried first to revive him, unable to believe what was happening, shouting for doctors who felt completely helpless when they came to examine the bleeding leader, crying in rage and anguish as they pronounced him dead. A few people placed their coats under him so he wouldn't lie on the hard cement and others covered his body to lend him some of their warmth.

A multitude gathered around the being who had been shattered by the bullets, some in silence but the majority shouting and swearing vengeance, their attention divided now between the body which still lay bleeding on the steps of the Senate and the murderer who had emptied his revolver to assassinate and who now screamed for mercy from behind that protective metal screen where he was able to ward off the blows he would have received, begging to be turned over to the police and tried in a court of justice as his victim would have wanted.

It was then, finally, after the five centuries of terror and injustice, when people carrying all sorts of weapons came down in a mad rush from all the filth-infested shacks of the surrounding hills, to join forces with the laborers who had dropped their work to form an increasing multitude in the plaza by the side of their slain leader, filling the surrounding streets and avenues with millions who kept pouring into the center of the city when they heard the news which passed through the darkest and most abandoned neighborhoods of the city from mouth to mouth, down on through the streets that emptied onto the plaza which became packed with those who arrived running and out of breath, who had so loved the deceased during his life and many of those who followed him wherever he spoke, men and women shouting and adolescents, screaming obscenities, who sold newspapers on the corners at dawn, just as he had done in his youth, and those who shined shoes and who now carried as their only weapons those small boxes of metal or hardwood that they decorated individually, where they kept the shoe polish, accessories and tools necessary in their occupation as bootblacks and when the workers poured out in disorder from the factories, quitting their jobs, running hurriedly, all of them arriving too late to help him and realizing that the one they most loved had ceased to exist, seeing him defeated on the cement and wondering in despair how could it be possible that this was the same man to whom they had entrusted their faith and hope, their own candidate, their friend and protector, their comrade, pronouncing his name with a desperate tenderness and when they heard that yes, this is him, this is the one, yes, the one they shot down and tossed aside here like bleeding garbage, the one the villains assassinated, the one they had finally murdered without giving him a chance as they always murdered, when they drew near to touch him, to caress him, to clean away the blood that ran all over the still warm body, they cried for him, yelling no, that it wasn't true, that it couldn't be, that their hopes couldn't die like this, and when the horror came over them, frightening them as they realized that perhaps without him their aspirations would also die here on the cement floor outside the Senate to which they had never had access but where their leader had given battle for them with his brave words, words which no one dared challenge because they spoke the truth, and the people heard them knowing always that if anyone could redeem them, if anyone could save their lives and their children's future it would be this man, with the assurance and confidence he always demonstrated, that smiling look of an understanding friend who knows pain and hunger, with those phrases with which he defended the poor, never failing to hit the mark, uncontainable fury welled up in their hearts.

When they realized that they were in imminent danger, in the midst of a terrible trap that would perhaps imprison them for another few centuries of disgrace and infringement of their rights, spreading terror among them before another person like this man who now lay helpless could spring again from among their ranks, when they thought that their longing, the promised dream which they had repeated like a holy prayer all their lives would be buried once again by the powerful with all the severity of hypocrisy and the new false promises they always made, and that the truly guilty ones would continue tormenting their children's children and the children of those who had not yet even been conceived, when they realized that now nothing would remain for them unless they stood up to fight for what was theirs, the total and instantaneous fury of the multitudes broke out with unbounded frenzy in thousands of destructive and rebellious acts in every corner of the nation as if a national accord had always existed among the oppressed.

There rose in them a secret but decisive pact to loot and burn the grocery stores that had always been beyond their reach, gulping down as much food as possible while they overturned automobiles and streetcars, while they broke down the doors of the mansions belonging to the owners of the city, and engaged in a merciless battle against all authority here in the plaza, where was found the eye of the human maelstrom that was now unleashed as people threw themselves headlong like a human avalanche, abandoning all trace of fear or caution, and attacked the cordon of police who had come to save the assassin and have him conveniently vanish so no one would ever find out who were the intellectual authors of the assassination and who, in the blinking of an eye, were completely subjugated and removed in spite of the many casualties, with the weapons that were ripped out of the soldiers' and policemen's hands, by the growing mob that finally rushed against the protective metal mesh with a furious thrust, attacking it with sticks and rocks and whatever else came within reach of their vengeful hands, shaking and finally knocking it down, entering the pharmacy to look for the vile assassin who was huddled fearing for his life behind one of the counters where he started to defend himself by raising his gun toward those who jumped on top of him, not quick enough to stop the ones who were already beating him with their shoeshine boxes and the others who were scratching him frantically and tearing off pieces of his clothing while others were biting his face and body, ripping pieces of his flesh with their teeth and kicking him until he finally ceased to resist and was transformed into an unrecognizable bleeding mass without even a scrap of clothing to conceal the deformed pieces of flesh that dangled haphazardly from his bones now ripped to bits by another wave of infuriated, shouting boys who continued the ferocious stomping of his organs scattered through the street where his eviscerated body had been dragged leaving a repugnant trail of blood and intestines as the detestable cadaver was pulled and pushed and kicked and decapitated, kicking the lacerated head like a football for several blocks toward the presidential palace in this macabre demonstration in which the assassinated leader was carried on the shoulders of the multitude following those who had given free reign to the feverish vengeance that culminated at the very doors of the presidential palace where the grotesque head first rolled toward the majestic portal and then was grabbed up by the hair that still remained on it and hurled by a gigantic man over the top of the high fence with the skill of a spectacular athlete who throws a discus to the winds at the height of his career in a world championship event with such remarkable accuracy that it hit the window of one of the bedrooms and, breaking the imported glass, bounced inside and finally disappeared never to be seen again while in the street a bloody battle was shaping up.

The army troops began to take up strategic positions from which they machine-gunned hundreds of people on that first day of a conflict that would last for decades and in which more than a million citizens of all ages would lose their lives, while the threatening tanks, generous gifts made in the name of democracy and freedom and sacred human rights by the same cynical foreigners who in the name of private enterprise came to shamelessly carry off half the nation's wealth, gifts and aid to that sonofabitch dictator who insisted on being addressed by everyone as His Excellency, the President of the Republic, those tanks which now appeared on the corners of the streets to disperse the rebellious crowd that nevertheless ventured to climb on top of the war machines, incapacitating them with gasoline bottle bombs and succeeding in capturing others with the help of soldiers who at the decisive moment chose to take off their vile uniforms and join with their people in revolt, were used to knock down the walls and parapets from which machine guns spread their devastation, toppling the buildings into ruins, dissolving them in that incendiary rage, in this apocalyptic strife that scourged the valley, reducing the burnt city to rubble and dust, taking the monopolists by surprise and trapping them with their arrogant complacency in their luxurious residences while other better organized guerrillas headed toward the armories in the army barracks to find and possess the weapons to engage the enemy in new struggles for liberation from the mountains of incomparable beauty to the hidden valleys, into the impenetrable jungles and in every corner of our beloved country wherever a vestige of tyrannous despots was to be found until the blessed day of their death when they would fall on the lovely earth they never loved, definitely and forever overthrown!

'Knowing our history and language as well or better than we do, from the most hidden depth of Berger-Kiss' narrative, he says: 'All of us are brothers. I am one of you. I suffer with you and write for you. I don't abandon you. With my pen I fight your battles. I know we shall win'. He has succeeded in writing a psalm of poverty, a hymn of the oppressed. He has portrayed us with great compassion, love and amazing literary skill."

Professor Germán Posada
National University, Colombia

"Andrés Berger-Kiss, although mischievously playful with dialects within Spanish, still adheres to a standard of linguistic purity where English is concerned, even though, spiritually, or psychologically, he has not left Colombia."

Professor Jonathan Tittler
Cornell University

"CHILDREN OF THE DAWN *is a sweeping, strong novel."*

Ellen Joseph
Houghton Mifflin Company

"Andrés Berger-Kiss, at home in many worlds, reflects the true culture of the late 20th century. He's a product of the Europe of his first years (Hungary and Holland), the Colombia of his childhood/early adulthood, the USA where he obtained a Ph.D., and especially Oregon, where he's lived for some three decades. Regular travel to Europe and Latin America, where he delivers his poetry recitals in Spanish and English at various universities, has heightened his links to these parallel universes.

"Children of the Dawn *reflects Berger-Kiss' turbulent connection with Colombia from the '30s to the '50s. Better than anything I've read or experienced, it explains the painful underpinnings of the heartland of the Colombian guerrilla movement and the* narco-traficantes *who've so shaped relations between our inextricably bound-up nations for the past 25 years."*

David Milholland
President, Oregon Cultural Heritage